MW00585955

SPECIAL EFFECTS

Jo Leigh

A KISMET™ Romance

METEOR PUBLISHING CORPORATION
Bensalem, Pennsylvania

To my mother and father, for all their love and support.

JO LEIGH

Jo Leigh worked in the motion picture business for many years before turning her hand to writing. She currently lives in Southern California with her husband, Brad, and her dog, Sparky.

ONE

All she had to do was get passed the dead body.

The noise from bursting cannon shells echoed in her ears and made it hard to think straight. Just a few more steps, then she could relax. If she moved a little to her left, she could hide behind the horses. No, they were more skittish than she was.

Catlin Clark ducked as another shell exploded nearby. In front of her lay the dead and wounded, and behind them, the cameras. For the moment, all she could do was figure out an escape plan . . . and plot her revenge. As the newest member of the movie crew, she'd been prepared for some kind of "welcome," but she'd never expected to be thrust smack into the middle of the Civil War!

The dirty skunks had dropped her off behind a wall of facades and told her that Mr. Peters, her new boss, was just around the corner. Very amusing. Not only was Mr. Peters nowhere in sight, she was in imminent danger of blowing this shot. With four

7

cameras rolling, hundreds of extras and the special effects, it would be far better to just die than stop the filming.

At least there was no physical danger. The bullets were blanks and the explosives were carefully marked. But on her first day as the associate producer, she'd wanted to make a good impression. Now, all she could hope for was to get out of this without looking like a fool and costing the film company several thousand dollars.

There was a lull in the firing, and she took advantage of the calm to peek around her enclosure. Yankees and Rebels ran helter-skelter across the dirt-strewn streets. The bloodied soldier lying a few feet in front of her winked and wiggled his nose.

Then everything happened at once.

The loudest explosion she'd ever heard crashed through the air and shook the earth. She practically jumped out of her skin, then grabbed the nearest wall and hung on. The horses went crazy and bucked and flung their legs wildly. With a last violent tug, they pulled out the post that anchored them to the ground.

And the little boy stood in the middle of the street.

Before she could think, she was moving. All she could see was the child standing frozen with terror. She felt the powerful horses next to her, heard their panicked breathing. They raced toward the child . . . and she knew she couldn't possibly win.

She flung herself in the path of the animals and grabbed the boy as she hit the ground. The horses swerved, missing her legs by inches. In a heartbeat, they were passed leaving only the echoes of their hoofbeats reverberating in her chest.

Then there was quiet, an unnatural stillness that

frightened her as much as the explosion had. Everything seemed to slow down to a crawl, even her own heartbeat. Somewhere a whistle blew, and the world started moving again.

The call went out for the medic. Then she heard a soft whimpering and was surprised to find out it was the boy crying and not herself.

"Are you okay?" she asked.

He nodded. Catlin sat up, cradling him and trying to control her suddenly racing pulse. She didn't even look at the crowd gathering around them. Gentle hands came down on her shoulders, others wrested the child from her grip. She was eased backwards until she lay on the dirt street.

Someone was talking, but it seemed as if the voice came from a million miles away. "I've got him."

She closed her eyes. Maybe the sick feeling in her stomach would ease, now that she knew he was being cared for. Her concentration shifted to her legs. Someone was touching her softly, tentatively exploring her limbs. It must be the medic, she thought, and she allowed herself to relax a bit. The hands moved up passed her knees to examine her thighs.

Although she was comforted by the human contact, she thought this exam might be more properly done in private. It was purely clinical, but she felt funny about a stranger touching her so . . . intimately. When his hand reached her groin, she opened her eyes. And stared at the most devastating man she'd ever seen.

He wasn't handsome. Striking? Rugged? No, he was just plain gorgeous. He was a big man. She could see that even though he was kneeling. His dark hair was slightly wavy and long enough to curl over his collar. With his chiseled good looks, he was more a romantic leading man than a set nurse.

Now the palm that rested just above her pubic bone was entirely too familiar. She tried to sit up, but his other hand, on her shoulder, kept her flat. All struggling ceased when he smiled and caught her in his gaze.

His eyes were blue—deep, rich, dark blue. His look held her captive long enough for her to notice how thick his black lashes were and that laughter had left lines etched like tiny crooked grins above his cheekbones.

"Don't even think about moving, okay?" His voice was low and rich. "Does anything hurt?"

"No. How's the boy?"

"He's fine. But he won't be after I get through with him. That kid's been a little terror ever since we started filming here." The man smiled warmly and moved his hands to her shoulders, gently forcing her to lie still. "But I'm glad he wasn't hurt. You did good."

Relaxing even further at his reassuring words, she closed her eyes for a moment and gathered her strength. "Thanks, doc. I can get up now."

His low chuckle made her look at him again. "What?" Just then, a small bearded man carrying a medical bag broke into the circle surrounding her.

"Well, well, what have we here? Someone hurt?" He sounded like Mr. Rogers.

Catlin stared at the medic, then glared at the man whose hand still rested casually on her stomach. "Seemed like a good time for a quick feel or what?"

He burst out laughing, his whole face joining in. "It *was* nice, but I've been trained in first aid. I have

to be. I'm Luke McKeever, the special effects man."
He looked up. "Nothing seems to be broken,
Julius."

"That's wonderful," the medic said. "But to be
sure, let me just take a quick look at her. Can she
walk over to my trailer?"

Before she knew what was happening, she was
lifted in the air and brought tight against the chest
of the special effects man. Blushing furiously, she
turned to glower at him. When she met his eyes, her
rage died, and she was shocked again at how his
gaze pierced her, probing and incessant. A new and
unexpected warmth surged through her as she experienced the closeness of their bodies. His powerful
arms accommodated her one hundred ten pounds as
if she were a feather.

The strange procession, which seemed to include
half the movie crew, filed passed the huge trucks and
equipment that covered the dirt-filled street, dressed
to look like the old South of the Civil War. Acutely
embarrassed at being the center of attention, Catlin
forced herself to look at the make-believe world that
had been created.

The Natchez, Mississippi, storefronts were all painted
and decorated in the style of the 1860s. The extras
appeared as if they had been born in Dixie: the
women looked like so many Scarlet O'Haras in their
hoop skirts and bonnets, and the men were resplen-
dent in their gray Confederate jackets.

Still cradled in the arms of a stranger, Catlin
watched as the crowd around them parted for an ex-
tremely short man of about fifty who shouldered his
way through the ragtag army. He was flushed; his

small gray eyes burned like bullets and his mouth was a taut line. She swallowed. It was Mr. Peters. Her boss.

She struggled to be released, but the arms around her felt like an iron bar. "Please, let me down. I'm fine," she pleaded, desperate to be on her feet.

"Is she hurt, McKeever?" Peters pointedly ignored her.

"Don't think so, but Julius needs to check her out."

"I'm fine!" she said. No one paid any attention to her.

"What the hell happened? I thought you had this shot under control." Peters glared at the man who held her captive. It was as if she had disappeared.

"Talk to the wrangler. The horses got loose. Almost trampled. . . ."

"What was she doing in the middle of the street? Don't I pay you people to make sure that kind of crap doesn't happen?"

Catlin stopped struggling, sure that every ounce of credibility was lost forever. "Mr. Peters, I assure you. . . ."

"Save it." With those words, he was gone, his clipped steps reminiscent of a general who'd lost the battle, but surely wouldn't lose the war.

What an ignominious introduction: She must look like a complete fool. Chalk one up for the new kid. Sighing heavily, she was grateful to enter the small mobile trailer, which held the offices of Julius Renquist, R.N. Luke set her down gently on the cold leather table dominating the modest room.

Before she could thank him, Julius chased him out

the door, clucking like a mother hen. Then he got down to the business of the examination.

"I'm not an M.D., you understand, but I am a fully qualified registered nurse. Can you take off your pants? We'll have a look at that leg." Sensitively, and with a thoroughness she admired, he examined her. And, with the exception of an ugly bruise, declared her fit for duty. With the briefest of thanks, Catlin dressed and rushed for the door, anxious to repair the damage caused by the morning's fiasco.

When she stepped out, she was greeted by four very large, very sheepish drivers. The same drivers who'd dropped her off in back of the facades this morning.

"Just wanted to say we're real sorry, ma'am," said the tallest. Was his name Jeff?

"Yeah. Hope you weren't hurt. It was just a little joke, see. We kind of initiate the new crew members . . ."

". . . didn't mean any harm. . . ."

". . . glad you saved the kid. . . ."

They were all talking at once. It was comical, seeing these big burly men—the smallest couldn't have been under six foot four—acting as if they'd broken a church window with their baseball. Well, she couldn't laugh. It was a mean, despicable thing they'd done. And besides, she hadn't figured out what she was going to do to retaliate yet. She wanted to do something slow and painful, but she'd probably settle for absconding with their evening beers.

Practical jokes were part of the territory, and she didn't want it getting around that she couldn't take them. This was her first film with this crew, and no matter what, she wanted to fit in. Of course, that was assuming she still had a job.

The men had stopped apologizing and were waiting for her to make her move. "I'm not going to forgive you, so you might as well go back to work."

Their crestfallen looks almost made her laugh out loud, but she held her mirth intact. "Go on, get away. I have to see if I still work here."

"Don't let Peters bully you. We'll tell him it was our fault."

"No thanks," she said, walking between two of the men. "I've had enough of your help for one day."

She was quite sure they couldn't see her smile.

"Well done."

Catlin stopped. That voice belonged to Luke McKeever. She took another step, then she saw him leaning against the door of a big rig where he was braiding a long cord of rope. Now that they were both vertical, she could properly assess the man who'd been so attentive.

Was there a height requirement on this film? All the men seemed to be giants, and Luke was no exception. The jeans he wore seemed to stretch forever between his scruffy, well-worn boots and his hand-tooled leather belt. Her gaze lingered over impossibly wide shoulders tapering to narrow hips. His shirt was gray denim and the sleeves were rolled up, exposing tan, muscled arms.

She could almost feel the strength ooze out of him. Despite his relaxed attitude, he seemed to be coiled as tightly as the rope he was working, ready to spring into action at a moment's notice.

Her gaze travelled upwards until she reached his face. She smiled self-consciously when she saw that he was giving her the same once-over she'd just given him. But just one look at those eyes, and she felt herself grow warm. Every fiber in her being was telling her to get away, and quickly, because this boy spelled danger.

He was just the kind of guy she could fall for. Not just because of his looks, although they certainly didn't hurt, but the humor flashing in his eyes, coupled with the gentleness she'd felt during his impromptu exam were the magical combination that sent her heart skittering. Yes, he was trouble, all right.

But she knew all about location romances. They happened to almost everyone. You lived with a small group of people for months. You ate, slept, worked, and played with the same folks, day after day. You picked the one you wanted, and that was it: instant romance. You were mad about each other until the plane ride home. Once you reached L.A., all bets were off.

Only she'd learned the rules too late, and she had the shattered heart to prove it. Never again would she fall for a guy on the road, especially one who was as smooth as Luke McKeever seemed to be.

So why was she shivering as she recalled the feel of his hands on her thighs? "I don't know whether to thank or slap you," she said.

His grin grew slowly until it overtook his eyes. "Both sound promising."

"Thanks."

"Damn."

"Really, thank you. But I can't chat now, I've got to go find Peters and see if I still work here."

"Ah, there are things you need to know about ol' Peters."

She'd started to walk past him, but he joined her and they moved toward the cameras at a fast clip.

"Like?"

"He's a ten-minute man."

"That certainly explains it all," she said with only a touch of exasperation.

"You always need to know everything in such a hurry?"

"When we're talking about the works of Shelley, you can take all the time you want. But when my career's under discussion, I get a little bit jumpy."

"Got it. Peters is the master of the ten-minute rage. He'll blow up, threaten whatever poor sucker's in his path with instant termination, then, about ten minutes later, he'll cool off and forget about the whole thing. Everyone who works with him for any length of time knows about his little quirks, but since this is your first day. . . ."

"So, I should just ignore this morning and hope he forgets that I blew a four-camera shot?"

Luke looked at his watch. "I'd ignore it for about three more minutes."

Catlin caught sight of her boss. He was standing next to the A camera, scowling. She stopped walking, and so did Luke. "I thank you for your advice, but running away from responsibility isn't my style."

Luke shook his head, and she made the mistake of looking into his eyes. In a flash, her job, her determination, even her name were obliterated from her mind, and all she could think of was how she'd never seen a blue that rich or that damned sexy. She tried to save herself by looking down, but then she saw his full lips slowly curve into an easy grin. How would those lips feel on her own? The thought was enough to jerk her back into the present, blushing furiously.

"Thanks again, but I gotta go." She turned quickly, trying to avoid another look at his face.

"Hey."

She stopped and took a deep breath. No, she wouldn't turn around. "Yes?"

"You never told me your name."

Just his voice was creating havoc in her stomach. She'd tell him and be off. "Catlin Clark." She took a step.

"I'm not finished with you, Catlin Clark. Not by a long shot."

Luke didn't move, he just watched Catlin cross the street. He couldn't seem to take his eyes off her backside. It was as enticing as the rest of her. With her flashing green eyes and luscious red lips, he'd found himself wanting to do a lot more than just talk. But there was something about her—was it a hint of fear behind the confidence?—that told him to take it easy. Catlin Clark was going to be a challenge.

He wasn't worried about her confrontation with Peters. She'd hold her own, just as she had with the drivers. Yeah, he thought, she'd be one tough negotiator. He looked forward to his turn. Since this show had so many special effects, he'd need to deal with her on a daily basis. It was his job to ask for money and hers to fight him about it.

He lifted the braided rope from the ground and made his way through the maze of equipment toward his truck. He had to prepare for the next battle sequence, which would take place that afternoon. What he really needed was more ammo. The local gunsmith had enough to fight three wars, but Luke hadn't been able to get the budget to buy all he wanted. Maybe his luck would change, now that Catlin was on board.

She'd probably have her hands full today, but maybe tonight would be a good time to drop by her room and talk about the kind of fireworks he wanted to make . . . on camera and off.

Catlin sank into her bathtub and groaned. The Epsom salts would help relieve the soreness she felt from top to bottom. Particularly bottom. The small room was steamy and the heat seeped into her body, easing the ache from her muscles and allowing her to relax for the first time since she'd spoken to Peters.

When she'd taken the job as an associate producer for Mandalay Productions, she'd replaced a man who'd worked for Eldon Peters for over ten years. He'd finally gotten a shot at producing his own television movie. That was *her* goal. She was determined to be a line producer by the time she was thirty. That left only four years.

This movie-of-the-week was a nice feather in her cap. She'd been working in the industry since she was eighteen, first as a clerk, then in accounting, and eventually as assistant to the producer of a highly-successful series. Two years ago, she'd gotten her first job as an associate producer. That had been followed by three pilots, two of which were filmed on location. In the last eight years, she had marched steadily up the ladder.

Even though she'd finally gotten Peters to accept her explanation of what had happened, she felt as if she would be on thin ice for a while. It was important for her to do an exemplary job because she wanted very badly to stay. It was odd that Peters came around about three minutes into the argument . . . just as Luke had predicted.

Suddenly, she was no longer thinking about her job or her boss. She was seeing a powerful body lean over her, feeling hands touch her intimately, watching incredible blue eyes fill with concern. She squirmed at the recollection, sending the bathwater over the edge of the tub. She would like to get to know Luke McKeever.

Special effects. He certainly had a special effect on her.

Leaving the comfort of the bath, Catlin grabbed a white towel from the rack and dried herself as she walked into the other room.

Was she crazy? McKeever was nothing but bad news. She knew men like him—great looking guys who knew how to take a girl's heart and break it into teeny tiny pieces. Hadn't she had her fill of "charmers" with Craig? And Luke was definitely a charmer. His smile alone made her all hot and bothered.

She'd just have to steel herself and make sure everything between them remained professional. That shouldn't be too hard. The job would surely keep her so busy that she'd have no time for anything else.

Her alarm said it was eleven o'clock already. She was exhausted, but she hadn't taken a break for dinner, so she was starving, too. It always took at least a week for her body to readjust to location hours.

An eleven P.M. dinner wasn't unusual. Neither was a four A.M. breakfast. But for four months she'd gotten used to eating and sleeping like a normal person in the real world, and her stomach was letting her know that the change wasn't a welcome one.

Maybe she could grab a quick sandwich before she went to sleep. She put on her old, comfortable sweats and ran a brush through her hair. Should she wear makeup? No, she was too hungry and tired to bother. Everyone was probably finished with dinner, anyway.

She tucked a few dollars into her waistband and headed toward the dining room.

"Hey, wait up."

Oh, no. Not him. Catlin looked down at her outfit: her sweatshirt had a giant bleach stain and the pants were torn at both knees. Even her tennis shoes were decrepit. This would teach her to rush out looking like a refugee. He'd see her and run screaming for the hills.

"Catlin. I was on my way to see you. I'd like to discuss a little business before morning."

She turned and smiled brightly. "To tell you the truth, Luke, I was just leaving. Maybe you could call me in half an hour?" *Please*, she begged silently, *please go away*.

"Where are you off to?"

He was standing too close. She took a step away from the harsh yellow light coming from the bulb hanging directly above her. "I, uh, was going to get a bite to eat." She pointed in the general direction of the lobby. "The dining room."

"You're too late. They close at ten. I've got an idea. Let's go to the market. I need to stock my shelves, and who knows when we'll have the next opportunity to shop. You have a fridge in your room, don't you?''

She nodded. ''I haven't had time to get anything to put in it yet.''

''Great, let's go.'' He placed his hand gently above her elbow. The soft touch was enough to make a shiver run down her arm.

''Wait. I have to get my purse.'' He dropped his hand, and she instantly felt more in control of the situation. Okay, all she had to do was make sure they didn't touch.

She unlocked her door, but didn't invite him in. ''I'll be just a second.'' Once she was safely inside, she grabbed a pair of jeans from her closet and struggled to get them on as she raced into her bathroom. She moaned as she looked at herself in the mirror. Could she look a little worse? Maybe if she blacked out some of her teeth. She had only a minute. Grabbing her mascara, she hardly watched as she brushed some on her lashes. That would have to do.

After collecting her purse, she left the safety of her motel room. Luke was leaning against the guard rail, whistling softly to himself. His lazy grin made her feel unexpectedly sexy, even though she knew she looked like hell. He walked her slowly to the parking lot, then opened the door to his pickup and helped her into the passenger seat. Each time he touched her, she felt her skin react with strange pleasure.

He climbed into the cab and gripped the gearshift, then eased the car into reverse. As he stepped on the gas, Catlin couldn't help but notice his thigh tense in his tight, worn jeans. The size of him was intimidating . . . but she'd cope.

They drove down some deserted country roads, back toward the center of town. She tried to see something of the countryside, but there were few streetlights to illuminate the view. She gave up the attempt and concentrated on Luke.

He was wearing a cologne she couldn't identify. It suggested woods and smoke and something else— some elusive essence that was distinctly male. What it did to her was very dangerous. The smell was somehow feral, and bypassed her mind to rouse a deeper part of her. It was as if his scent stimulated the animal being she'd been socialized to hide. She breathed deeply and had an almost uncontrollable urge to growl.

She rolled her window all the way down and took a huge breath of magnolia-scented night air. Was she nuts? All this fuss over a scent? No. She'd better keep her priorities clearly in mind. Work came first, second, and last.

He turned onto the main highway. At the next stop sign, he looked at her and smiled. Staring deep into her eyes, he gunned the motor and put the pickup in gear. Then, he leisurely turned his attention to the road, leaving her even more unsettled.

"Um, are there any stores open this late?" she asked.

"I'm going to introduce you to the wonders of the Piggly Wiggly," he answered, smiling.

"Piggly Wiggly?" She laughed. "What, pray tell, is that?"

"Oh, it's just like any supermarket in L.A., but I get a kick out of the name. They sell everything but the kitchen sink."

"I can't wait," she said. "I'll keep an eye out for

Henny Penny and Georgie Porgie.'' Catlin caught herself staring at the angles of his face that were illuminated by the lights of the dashboard. ''Have you been here long?''

''Two weeks.'' He turned left, letting his hand glide over the wheel with just the barest of contact. ''I came on board during the first week of pre-production. I've been working on the Atlanta scene all this time. I've also turned into something of a baby-sitter. That kid, Brandon, you saved. He and his friends spend just about every day hanging out on the set. No one has the heart to kick them out, they love it so much. But after today, they won't be allowed near us unless we're filming only dialogue.''

''That's a relief. I don't mind telling you I aged a good five years this morning. And I can't afford that again.''

Luke looked at her appraisingly. ''I don't know. You look mighty young to me.''

''If that's your delicate way of asking my age, forget it. Hey, didn't you say you had some business to discuss?'' she asked.

''Nice dodge. But I'll bite anyway. After the way you handled those drivers, I sure don't want to tangle with you. Seriously though, I'll be needing more ammo. My budget hasn't, um, technically been finalized, and I was wondering. . . .''

''Hold it right there, slick. The one thing I did get to do before coming out here was review the budget. I seem to recall special effects getting a very large piece of the pie.''

''Not that big.''

''Luke, this isn't a feature. There isn't any more money to give you.''

"There's always more."

She didn't say anything for a moment. "There is one place where I might be able to finagle some money."

"Yeah?"

"I could take some from your salary."

He laughed. "Uncle. At least for now."

He pulled into the parking lot of the brightly lit Piggly Wiggly market. Luke opened the door for her, taking her hand in his. For a moment, he held it, and the feel of his thumb rubbing against her palm made her shiver. Then he let it go, and she quickly shoved her hands in her pockets as they walked into the store. She grabbed a cart and they started perusing the goods.

"This looks tasty." Catlin pulled out a large jar of pickled pig's feet. "Might be good with a claret, or perhaps a full-bodied Bordeaux."

"How can you say that?" he said, his demeanor completely serious. "Some of my closest friends are pigs."

She giggled and put the jar back on the counter. He looked as if he wanted to tell her something, but then he just smiled at her. His grin was kind of crooked, as if something odd had just occurred to him.

"What?"

"Nothing."

She didn't believe him for a minute. Unfortunately, no nursery rhyme characters were shopping, only ordinary housewives and a few people in business clothes. She got some aspirin, bottled water, and other items she would need. He loaded up on cookies, candy, and soda.

"How can you eat that much junk and not blow up like a balloon?" she asked.

"I have the metabolism of a racehorse. Millions hate me, but my other charms make up for it."

"Oh. And when will I be seeing them?"

"Touché. You may be laughing now, but don't say I didn't warn you. Soon, you, too, will be swept away by my mesmerizing ways."

She turned and studied a box of oatmeal. Judging by the way her insides were doing flip-flops, it might already be too late. He was as charming a man as she'd ever met. This kind of reaction to someone she'd only known one day was downright crazy. Maybe her fall had been more serious than she thought. Perhaps these feelings were all caused by brain damage.

At the produce section, things got worse. He wanted some melons, so they squeezed the ripe crenshaws and honeydews. As she watched his large hands gently press the skin of the fruit, she imagined him exploring her body with the same sensitivity. A shudder ran through her, settling in her breasts. She left him, and moved over to safer fruit.

By the time Catlin got back to her motel room, it was after midnight. She emptied the bag from the market and changed her clothes. She put on a ridiculous T-shirt that said PIGGLY WIGGLY under a large, grinning pig emblazoned on the front. It was a gift from the crazy special effects man.

He was so terrific that she found herself worrying. No one is that great, she thought. He probably lives with his mother, or dresses in women's clothing.

She giggled. The thought of that big hunk of a

man in a frilly dress was absurd, but she knew there had to be something wrong with him.

She was not about to be caught unawares this time. That had happened before. She'd loved Craig with all her heart, and she'd believed he'd loved her. He'd been her perfect match. Together, they'd planned a wonderful life, complete with 2.4 children and a house with a picket fence.

Then, the movie ended. And with it, their relationship. Despite all his declarations of love, she'd been just another location romance. Well, that wouldn't be a problem with Luke. Not only was any kind of relationship totally out of the question, she would be far too busy concentrating on her work to pay any attention to the man.

After brushing her hair, she went into the bathroom to wash her face. That's when she saw it. A great glob of black mascara smeared below her right eye. Maybe he hadn't seen it, she thought desperately. Maybe it had just happened. And then she remembered his odd little grin at the supermarket.

Perfect, she thought. Grace Kelly strikes again.

TWO

Catlin sat bolt upright in her bed, grabbed her alarm clock and threw it across the room. It was no use. The damn thing wouldn't stop screeching. After a long, low groan, she struggled to her feet and shuffled across the floor to pick it up. Four a.m. What an ungodly hour to start the day. Let's see, she thought, that would make three and a half hours of sleep. Great. With a heavy sigh and a shrug, she bowed to the inevitable. Maybe a shower would help revive her. If not, she would simply drown herself.

The shower was somewhat successful. After putting on a minimum of makeup and drying her hair, she struggled into jeans and a T-shirt. Finally awake enough to be nervous about seeing Peters, and perhaps even more nervous about seeing Luke, she gathered her notebook and purse, then headed to the lobby.

Downstairs, she was met by a group of sleepy wardrobe people struggling with heaps of freshly cleaned costumes. An attractive woman with tightly cropped gray hair was holding a pile of clothes that dwarfed her tiny body.

"Can I help?" Catlin asked.

Without a word, the diminutive woman dumped the entire mound of clothes in her arms. "Thank God. My arms were about to come out of their sockets." She looked at Catlin's stunned expression and burst out laughing. "Don't worry, I'll take them back. I just need to rearrange them. I'm Sylvia."

"Hi, I'm Catlin," she said, struggling under the weight of the bundle in her arms. "I'm the new associate producer."

Sylvia lifted one piece of wardrobe at a time and placed them neatly on the front desk. "Good luck," she said sardonically. "You'll have fun working with Peters. He's a real peach. This is my fourth Mandalay production. I can hear that man yell in my sleep. If you need help, I always keep a bottle of sherry in my room. Feel free."

The front door of the motel opened and a burly giant of a man sauntered in. He was wearing jeans that rode well below an enormous beer belly and a T-shirt that advertised his favorite brand. "All aboard," he bellowed. "First stop, Tearose Plantation."

Nudging Catlin, the wardrobe woman said, "That's our ride. Better not miss it. The next one won't be around for an hour." She grabbed the massive pile of clothes and made her way out to the mini-van parked directly in front of the motel.

"You comin'?" the driver asked.

Catlin was about to nod her head when she saw

Luke's truck pull up behind the van. He jumped out and walked into the lobby.

"Need a ride, lady?"

His sparkling smile made her weak in the knees. "Why, thank you. That would be nice."

The big man looked at her and grinned. "Be careful, honey. Those effects guys are hell on wheels."

"Thanks for the warning." She breezed out the door and Luke helped her into the front seat.

"Well, sunshine," Luke said lightheartedly, "ready to face another day?" He clambered in behind the wheel.

"How can you possibly be so cheerful this early in the morning?" Surprised to find herself suddenly feeling so chipper, she sought an easy explanation. Nerves, she thought. *I'm probably full of adrenaline.* The fact that Luke had picked her up couldn't have anything to do with it. After all, what harm could there be in just catching a ride?

She turned to study him in the light of the new day. He was as handsome as she remembered. His blue eyes were filled with an excitement that was palpable. She wondered if it was the job, or something else that made them glow. His jeans and work shirt were old, but clean, and his hair was still damp from the shower. Her stomach tightened as she inhaled his mysterious cologne again.

"You are going to Tearose, aren't you?" Luke asked as he turned out of the motel parking lot.

"Yep. I need to hook up with Peters."

"He doesn't show up until the director's on the set, which gives me time to show you around. I'm rigging for the next battle scene. I have four hundred guns to load with blanks, and seventy explosions to set up. It should be a hundred and twenty. . . ."

"I thought we discussed this last night," she said quickly.

"But I didn't really explain the situation properly. You see, what we've got here is a Civil War without enough bang."

"Oh? Is there a minimum bang that goes with each war, or just a general bang quotient?"

Luke's eyes narrowed and he shot her a sly grin. "Each and every battle has its own unique feel. And sound."

"And we're not loud enough."

He shook his head. "Not even close."

She stared out the front window. It was tempting to give in. He was so convincing, and he obviously cared so much. But what would that do to her budget? And how would Peters react if she increased the special effects so soon after arriving? "Sorry, Luke. I'd really like to help you out. . . ."

"Will you just think about it? At least until you've had a chance to see what I mean?"

She shrugged. "Sure. No harm in thinking."

"Great. I'll introduce you to Bessie and show you how we choreograph battle scenes. Give you some first-hand knowledge of the big-bang theory."

"I'm all atwitter. And who's Bessie?"

"Bessie isn't a who," he said. "She's my truck. Been with me for the past eight years. She's a beautiful five-ton with all my gear loaded in her. I can live in her, if necessary. She's got a fridge, a bed, and a hot plate."

The pickup slowed and they turned onto a dirt

road. "Here we are. Tearose Plantation. Built in 1836."

Catlin stared with awe at the beautiful antebellum mansion and the magnificent grounds shimmering in the first light of dawn. Towering willow trees covered with Spanish moss shaded the well-kept lawns. A large pond glimmered just off the dirt road. Two elegant swans were gliding gracefully across the still water. The air was thick with a perfumed mist, and she was enveloped in the heady scent of blooming magnolias. The glistening columns of the stately mansion bore mute testament to a hundred years of tradition. The history of the house, the cotton plantation, and the Old South were coming to life before her eyes.

"I didn't know it would be this beautiful," she whispered. "It's like a storybook. I just know Rhett Butler is going to come riding up. . . ."

At that very moment, the honey-wagon, which housed the bathrooms for the crew, rumbled around the corner, shattering the silence and her rosy image. They both laughed and she slugged him playfully on the shoulder. "Come on. Some of us have to work for a living."

He revved up his pickup and sped around the huge truck, his deep, hearty chuckle as comforting as a warm blanket.

As they drove onto the vast lawn, she saw vehicles, trailers, and equipment covering the beautiful grounds of the plantation. Wardrobe racks were standing next to tents marked GUYS and GALS. A large crowd was gathered in front of the catering truck, waiting for coffee. Everyone was wearing the traditional outfit for working on movies: jeans and T-shirts. Luke stopped and pointed to a huge white truck parked next to a double trailer. "That's Bessie."

It looked just like any other effects truck to her, but when Catlin glanced back at Luke, the gleam in his eyes told her Bessie was very special, indeed. "I'd love to see her."

He parked next to Bessie and jumped down from his seat. Charming her with his courtesy, he jogged around to her door and helped her down. The butterflies in her stomach did a soft-shoe as he guided her forward. He grabbed her around the waist and lifted her onto the open tailgate, which stood about a foot off the ground. His large hands nearly spanned her entire waist, and she relished the feeling of his strength. He hopped up next to her.

"Hey, Luke."

The boy's voice was coming from under the tailgate.

"It's Brandon," Luke explained, then he called down to the boy. "You come up here and say thank you to the lady who saved your butt."

The child crept out. He was only about eight or nine, she guessed, with big green eyes, an unruly mop of blond hair, and a smile filled with mischief. His overalls were faded blue with permanent grass stains on the patched knees. He had Band-Aids on both hands and each elbow. His smile faded as he saw Luke's harsh stare.

"Don't you have something to say, young man?" Luke asked.

"Yes, sir. Thank you, ma'am. It was real nice of you to save me from them horses." Brandon stared at the ground, scuffing the dirt with a worn tennis shoe.

Catlin had a hard time keeping a straight face. Not only was the boy as adorable as he could be, his Southern accent was utterly charming. Every word seemed to have twice the number of syllables she was used to. She felt as if she should be waving a fan and sipping a mint julep.

"What else?" Luke wasn't letting up. His voice was stern, and the boy straightened his spine before he went on.

"I'm sorry I caused so much trouble. I'll be real good from now on."

"Na own." She repeated the words to herself, just as he'd said them. She liked the way the Mississippi folks talked . . . tawked.

"I accept your apology, Brandon. My name's Catlin. If you want to watch us film, you come to me and I'll make sure you're in a nice, safe place. Okay?"

His face broke out in a dazzling smile. "You bet. My buddies, too?"

"Yes, you can bring your friends. But you must follow the rules. If you can't behave, then you can't watch."

"Yes'm."

He shot across the lawn, his little legs flying like the wind, but stopped suddenly and ran back to the truck. "Thank you," he gasped. Then he was off again.

"You've just signed up for a lot of trouble," Luke said. "Those kids will hound you until you want to strangle them."

"That's okay. Who knows, maybe Brandon will

turn out to be the next Spielberg or Lucas. And besides, if they get too unruly, I'll send them to you.''

"Gee, thanks." Luke grinned. "Now, let's take a look at Bessie." He bowed with a flourish and she turned to look inside.

The truck's interior was a jumble of wire, metal, and unidentifiable objects. Gun cases lay in front of large metal cabinets that had hundreds of small drawers. An old coffee pot sat on a hot plate that was fixed to the side of the truck. Stereo speakers were attached to all four upper corners. There were strange and dangerous looking tools scattered haphazardly over the floor. It looked like a giant version of the bottom of a very messy closet.

One side even had whole walls, painted to match the exterior of the plantation house, stacked neatly, one next to the other. When he caught her looking at them, he grinned proudly. "Those beauties are built to burn. We'll put them in front of the real house and torch them. You won't be able to see that it's only make believe.''

"I've never worked on a movie with special effects. All my shows have been bedroom dramas.''

"Well then, you have a lot to learn.'' He hurriedly shoved a case of bullets to the side of the truck with his foot, allowing her to walk deeper into the interior. He pointed to a thick piece of wood with electrical wires sticking out in a mass of red, blue, and yellow. The board itself had small numbers from one to fifty next to each wire.

"For example, that's a bullet board. Each one of those wires is connected to a hidden explosive at the other end. We can put them in walls or directly on to people. When the actor points his gun and pulls the trigger, I sit at the board and fire each hit. It looks as if he's shooting real bullets, but actually, they're blanks. We control all the action from behind the camera.''

Luke saw the mess on the cot and quickly moved over to straighten it up. "Why don't you look around? We'll be able to sit down in a minute.''

Catlin wandered to the back of the truck, looking at all the tools of his trade, but searching for more personal belongings. Other than a coffee cup stating EFFECTS MEN DO IT EXPLOSIVELY, there was nothing to give her any real insight into him.

But wait, was that lace? She glanced back quickly to see if Luke was watching her, but he was busy straightening the cot. She moved some papers aside. What would the special effects man need with a . . . garter? She picked up the satin garment from the counter top. It was scarlet with lace trim, and the letter H was embroidered on the front. H?

"Catlin?"

She dropped the garter on the counter and whirled around, then quickly joined Luke in the front of the truck. He took her hands and pulled her down with him onto the cot. "Well. What do you think?" He looked at her with an innocent, little-boy grin.

"It's nice," she said. *Could that garter be a prop?*

"Thanks. I built almost everything in here myself. Well, Stan and I built it."

"Stan?" she asked. Stan was definitely not a girl's nickname.

"Yeah, he's my assistant. You two haven't met yet. He's a great kid. You'll like him. He's been with me on my last two pictures."

She wondered who else had been with him . . .

perhaps a young lady who was missing one garter? Extricating her hand from his, she looked at her watch. "I have to go. I can't afford to be even a minute late. I have no idea what Peters has in store for me today."

"Whatever it is, I'm sure you'll handle it beautifully. But good luck, anyway."

"Thanks."

"Maybe we can get together for lunch? There's something else I want to show you."

"Maybe." *Watch out,* the little voice inside her head was screaming. *You already like this guy too much. And he owns one too many garters.* "I'll probably be busy with Peters, though. If there's time, I'll come by."

"Fair enough."

Luke helped her down. Before she turned away, she thought about the garter. He worked with a partner. The garter probably belonged to Stan's girlfriend. Yeah. That's it.

Peters was standing in front of the catering truck, sipping a steaming cup of coffee. He was dressed like the rest of the crew in jeans, T-shirt, and boots. His uniform, however, looked as if it were from Neiman Marcus, whereas the crew had probably gotten theirs at Sears.

Before she approached him, she took one last look at Luke, who was walking toward the main house. His stride was long and his gait masculine. He waved at the men unloading the cable, and they responded with friendly nods. Just before he reached the porch, he turned and looked directly at Catlin. A blush covered her cheeks as she realized that he'd guessed she was watching him.

She quickly turned back to her boss. "Mr. Peters." She put out her hand, but he didn't even glance at it.

"I want to go over the shooting schedule and the day-out-of-days with you." He gave her a hard, cold look. "I'm aware that you have some experience and I've been assured, by people I trust, that you can handle this job. They'd better be right."

He put his cup down on the long wooden table that was laden with fruit, donuts, and coffee accouterments, and started walking briskly toward a double trailer parked in back of the catering truck. Although she was longing for the food and drink, Catlin scurried to catch up with him. Not sure what he expected of her, she knew she'd better learn fast. She caught up with him as he opened the door.

Peters sat down at the circular table in the middle of the luxuriously appointed room. A quick glance told her it was used by only the top brass, because it was equipped with every amenity. A color TV was mounted on the wall across from the microwave oven and full kitchen unit. The upholstery was rich velvet and the carpet flowed across the lavish trailer like mint-green fur. The beautiful Monet landscape prints reinforced the serenity of the mobile oasis.

The contrast between the jumbled, cluttered truck she had just left and this elegant mobile home was so great it made her head spin. The work on the table was the only hint that this wasn't a pleasure craft. Covered with script pages of all colors, a computer, and a large cardboard folder, it brought her back to the work at hand.

Peters opened a folder and pointed to one of the many long, thin strips held inside. "This is today's work. We should be able to complete all of this crap by seven tonight. Tomorrow will be tougher because we have a company move."

The conversation became more technical, and she took copious notes and asked questions as they went along. After going over the day-out-of-days, she felt confident enough to follow the work on the set and know what was going on.

The day-out-of-days told her what actors worked when and their method of payment. Some were contract players, some were one-day, and others were three-day players. Each type was covered by a separate contract and, because they were so costly, it was important that they only worked for their allotted time. Overtime for actors was prohibitively expensive, and one of her jobs would be to see that no one worked longer than twelve hours out of twenty-four.

Peters told her about an actor who'd been replaced, and asked her to fill out the paperwork. With the new man playing Edward, they were saving almost two thousand dollars. She'd need to keep at least half of that money in the acting budget, but, maybe now, she could give Luke a break and pass on a few bucks to special effects.

Peters finally grabbed his briefcase and left her alone in the trailer. She sat a moment trying to organize her thoughts. The array of facts, timetables, and contracts that filled her mind could not still the sneaky interloper who wouldn't leave her alone.

Luke's strong back, his eyes, his sensual mouth, and, above all, that shiny red garter, stole into her musings even when she knew she should concentrate only on the work. This wouldn't do. There was a time and place for everything. This was the time for work and her place was on the set. Gathering her notes, Catlin left the trailer, determined to keep her mind on her job.

Luke jumped down from the tailgate of his truck and stretched his aching muscles. He needed to check with the prop department about some shoulder holsters, but he didn't feel like rushing. He decided to walk—the long way.

He couldn't keep his mind off Catlin. She had been so beautiful and helpless lying in the middle of the dirt-covered street—was it just yesterday? There was something startling in his reaction to her. He recalled her brown flowing hair, which made him think of liquid mahogany, her green eyes sparkling with an inner fire, and her soft, full mouth. His chest had tightened when he had touched her back and her slim hips. It had been hard to let go.

When his divorce had come through two years ago, he'd made the decision that permanent relationships and Luke McKeever didn't mix. Life on the road made it easy to be true to his credo.

There were always plenty of opportunities for meeting women on location. He hadn't missed many chances—one at a time, of course—and when the show ended, he was history.

But no one had ever captured his attention like Catlin. Her laugh, her smile, her voice all mesmerized him. He longed to know more about her, and to tell her about his life and his dreams. But he had a funny feeling she wasn't as anxious to know him.

He'd detected a wariness before she'd left Bessie. Was it his job, the fact that he was only the special effects guy, and not some bigwig?

Somehow, that didn't seem right. She'd been too nice last night. Walking through the aisles at the store, he'd felt as if they'd known each other for years. There were none of those awkward pauses that creep into most conversations with new acquaintances. She'd been open about herself and had acted interested in him. And she'd laughed at his jokes. That was a big plus.

He'd try again. He had a strong hunch that the lady who'd knocked him for a loop was destined to be the woman of his dreams . . . at least for a few months.

Perhaps he should send some flowers. No, better to just take his time and watch for an opening. Let her make the next move. Patience would win out.

As he wandered across the wide lawn, he looked at the producer's trailer. The door was shut tight. Patience, he thought once again. All good things come to those who wait.

"Action."

Sitting in her chair by the camera, Catlin watched Ken Vogel, the director, work his way through scene after scene. It wasn't hard to become engrossed in the intricacies of transforming the written word into a live-action drama. This setup had only two actors, both of whom knew their lines and hit their marks. Even so, they had to have coverage of the two of them together, a close-up of each one and medium shots for editing. After a few hours, she felt assured enough to voice her opinions, and was delighted when they were given full credence. The rest of the morning sped by.

Lunch was called. She had no idea where Luke was, which was good. She should go talk to other crew members, get to know a few more people. She'd just walk by his truck on her way to the caterer.

She passed by the wardrobe trailer and waved to Sylvia.

"How are you?" the woman called.

"Fine."

"Want to grab some chow with me?"

Catlin glanced at Bessie, then back at Sylvia. "I, um. . . ."

The older woman smiled. "No problem. I'd prefer to eat lunch with Luke, too."

Catlin felt herself flush. "What makes you think I'm going to see Luke?"

Sylvia walked down the three steps that led from her trailer. "Oh, honey, because he's about the best looking thing in long pants. If I were you, I would be on him like lint on velvet. Well, have a good one."

Catlin watched the wardrobe woman walk toward the long tables set out for the crew's lunch. What a character. It was going to be an interesting film.

People bustled by her, and even during lunch there was a buzz of activity all around. When she finally reached Luke's truck, she didn't see him or his pickup. Perhaps he'd gone into town.

She peered inside Bessie's darkened interior, and froze when she heard Luke's deep voice. She couldn't make out who he was talking to, but it was obviously a woman.

"Please, baby. I bought you a garter. Doesn't that mean anything to you? Let me put it on."

Then she heard the woman squeal in delight.

"Oh, Harriet, my love. You look good enough to eat." Then Luke laughed. She couldn't make out the next sounds she heard; they were probably muffled because he was kissing her.

Catlin shook as she ran all the way back to the production trailer. Harriet. So, while he was being so nice to her, Harriet was waiting in the wings. That . . . that slime. How dare he play her for a fool.

Wait a minute. What if he was just a nice guy, and she'd imagined his attraction out of wishful thinking? No, she wasn't that dense. He'd come on to her. And she *was* a fool. When would she ever learn?

Right now, she decided. For all intents and purposes, Luke was just another crew hand, and that was that. She sat down heavily on the padded couch. Thank heavens she'd learned about him so quickly. Why, she might have made a terrible mistake. Now, she could forget all about him.

She looked at her watch. It was still lunch. She should go out and eat with the crew, maybe find Sylvia and chat. But then she might see. . . .

The tiny freezer compartment of the trailer's refrigerator was packed with TV dinners. The turkey dinner was the easiest to extract, so she placed the container in the microwave and sat down at the table.

She glanced at her crew list, then tossed the paper aside. No. She wouldn't think about it any more. The seconds ticked by slowly, the silence of the trailer expanding until she could practically feel it. She began to hum and stood up to check the microwave.

It was by accident that she looked at the crew list again. No one was named Harriet. She looked through the cast list. Nope. Okay, so she was a local. That garter was pretty small. Harriet must be real petite. And probably wowed by a Hollywood special effects man. She'd be sweet and Southern and charming, and wouldn't know that she couldn't trust men. Poor thing.

The timer went off and Catlin got her meal. Poor thing, hah! She was probably a witch, and had ensnared Luke in a relationship he didn't even want. That made more sense. Luke was such a nice guy he probably didn't know what had hit him.

Yeah, and cows fly. She pierced the plastic cover of the small tray and allowed the steam to dissipate before she took a bite. Then she only nibbled at the unappetizing meat and potatoes. She must not have been as hungry as she thought.

Dammit, she was going to go meet this Harriet person, and get over Luke once and for all. She didn't even want a relationship with him, and here she was acting like a jealous idiot.

There was still ten minutes of lunch left. She got up, slammed the door of the trailer shut, and walked purposefully across the lawn toward Luke's truck. In front of the tailgate stood a gangly young man with a long blond ponytail and three earrings shimmering from one ear. His tank top was cropped and exposed an overly tan, washboard stomach. The shorts he was wearing were riding so precariously low on his hips that if he hiccuped he'd lose them. This, she thought, had to be Luke's partner, Stan.

"Hi. I'm Catlin. Associate producer." She extended her hand.

"Yo. Stan. Special effects."

"Nice to meet you."

"You're the chick Luke was telling me about. You almost got creamed yesterday." Stan laughed, a loud, earsplitting burst.

"Yes, I'm that chick all right," she replied.

"Heard you took a tour of ol' Bessie today. Great, ain't she?" Stan took a deep drink of the milk he was holding.

"Wonderful."

"Did you meet ol' Harriet?"

Catlin tried to keep her expression calm. "No, I haven't had that pleasure. Has Luke been seeing her for a long time?"

"Seeing her?" For some unknown reason, Stan laughed again. He was literally holding his sides. "Yeah, for about two years. They're quite an item. Hey, Luke," he yelled, "she wants to know how long you been seein' Harriet."

"Who?" His voice came from inside the truck. It was soon followed by his body. He'd taken off his shirt. His chest was muscled and lightly peppered with dark hair. Her mouth went dry as she watched him wipe off the thin sheen of sweat that made his skin shimmer. He'd been working hard . . . at something. She could guess what . . . or who . . . had made him perspire.

"Catlin. Great, I'm glad you're here. Come on up."

Before she could protest, Stan was handing her up to Luke, as if she were a piece of furniture. "I'm not crippled. I can get on a tailgate."

Stan thought that was hilarious, too.

"Now, what's all this about me and Harriet?"

Luke hadn't let go of her waist. She stepped away from him. "I was just wondering how long you two have been seeing each other. I'm sorry, if that's too personal. You don't have to answer."

Luke got that grin again, just like at the Piggly Wiggly. Her hand automatically went up to her eyes and she felt for her stray mascara.

"I think you two better meet." He took her hand and led her to the front of the truck. There was a door she hadn't seen before. He opened it and they walked down some wooden steps. She was standing in a small pen. A pink doghouse was set up, and next to that was a small puddle of muddy water. There was also an empty bowl on the ground.

Her cheeks started to burn. Harriet was a dog?

"Harriet, sweetie," Luke called softly.

Just then a baby pig, its little black belly almost touching the ground, came hurrying out of the doghouse. A pig? And she was wearing the red garter around her neck.

"That's Harriet?" she said in a very tiny voice. She was embarrassed and relieved, all at the same time.

"The lady in question. She's a Vietnamese pot-bellied miniature. She's fully grown, and quite a beauty, don't you think?"

Luke bent down and scooped her up in his arms. She was lying on her back, her four little piggy legs wiggling in delight as he scratched her belly.

Catlin couldn't help it. She started to laugh. The more she thought about her mistake, the funnier everything got. "I thought . . . That's Harriet." She wiped her eyes. Then she remembered the pickled pig's feet, and she cracked up again. "Oh, this is too much. But why a pig?"

"You can't travel with a dog because they bark. They can ruin shots. But she's not just *a* pig. She's Harriet, the stunt pig."

"Excuse me?"

"Harriet's an old pro at movies, aren't you, love?"

The pig gave a little grunt of satisfaction. He was tickling her under her chin, and she was obviously in hog heaven.

Catlin needed to sit down. Her side ached from laughing so hard. She went over to the steps.

"You want to hold her?"

"Sure, why not?"

Luke put her in Catlin's arms, just as if the animal was an infant. Harriet was staring at her with little pink eyes. She even felt like a baby. She was adorable. All warm and cuddly; her skin was as soft as a puppy's belly.

"She can swim, and doesn't get scared around explosions, so she's been in a lot of shots with other farm animals, but she's always the best. We're gonna use her in this one."

"Luke, she's great." The expression on his face reminded her of how her father looked when he was telling his buddies about his own daughter. Yep, she thought. This was a man who needed kids. "I love the garter."

"Well, she needed to get into the whole spirit of the movie. She'll be in a dance hall, you know."

Catlin just nodded, then went back to tickling Harriet. She was very endearing. Any man who could love this adorable creature couldn't be all bad. Then she remembered the time. "I've got to get back to work."

Luke took his pet from Catlin's arms and gave Harriet a kiss on the forehead. "See you later, sugar." He put her down.

Catlin could've sworn the pig wagged her little tail.

Back in the truck, Luke took her hand. "What are you doing about dinner tonight?"

"I don't know. I have no idea when I'll be getting off work." She liked having her hand held by him. It felt so safe. He'd managed to take all her silly fears and put them to rest, but dinner? Did she dare?

"Come to the restaurant at the motel. I've got another surprise for you."

"You don't have a pet elephant, do you?"

He laughed. "No. Seriously, I'd really like to see you. I'll meet you about nine?"

"If I can, I will. I promise. Now, I gotta run."

He let go of her. She walked slowly toward the tailgate.

"Don't order the pork ribs," Luke called.

She giggled and jumped down, unaided, from the truck.

"So, how'd you like ol' Harriet? She's a real bombshell, ain't she?"

"Stan, she's a knockout."

The two of them grinned at each other. He looked so out of place, here on a Southern plantation. He should be surfing in California. Catlin decided she liked ol' Stan.

"See you later," she said.

"Yeah. Later, dude. I mean, Catlin." The air was

once again filled with his laugh, then he went back
to loading muskets. Catlin just shook her head and
walked away.

What a pair. Luke and Stan. Luke and his pig.

Luke and Catlin?

That could be a dangerous combination. Was it
already too late? Was she destined to get hurt once
again? All she knew was that she was going to meet
him that night. At least they could be friends. And
if he wanted something more? She'd just have to set
him straight.

_____ THREE _____

The bar was dark and cool, and the music from the Wurlitzer filled the room with soft, hot jazz. Catlin spotted an empty table and sank gratefully into the overstuffed leather chair. Deep, calming breaths released the tension of her day and let her senses take over. The delicious fragrance of seafood and spices wafted in from the kitchen. A small candle on the table threw flickering lights across her motionless hands as the antique fan gently stirred the air.

It was just nine o'clock, and Luke was nowhere in sight, so Catlin turned her attention to the menu. She decided to start with some wine. A waitress took her order and left her alone again.

Looking around, she saw that the only customers were members of the crew. It seemed as though they had all chosen their partners already, for at each table there were couples or foursomes. It wasn't possible that they had been paired up before the movie began. This was proof, once again, about how common location romances were. She shook her head. Not for Mrs. Clark's daughter. No, sir.

After a friendly nod at a makeup man, she closed her eyes. As unpleasant as the truth was, she had to face up to it. Luke was just another location lothario. Sweet, yes; interesting, no question about it; but he was also a man who'd been working on the road for a lot of years. There was no doubt in her mind that he knew the ropes. With his looks, he'd have no trouble finding a temporary sweetheart in every state. What woman wouldn't fall for a guy who loved a pig?

She smiled, but she couldn't shake her melancholy. Maybe she was being a fool. If she wanted to be a producer, then she'd have to be on the road for the next several years. No man in a normal line of work would put up with that. And, if—and it was a very big if—she was to fall for a guy on the road, she knew it would only be politically correct for her to be with someone "above the line," such as another producer, director, or actor. Hollywood was a very small town with its own caste system. She'd been around enough to know people cared about that kind of thing. But did she?

A loud clang brought her attention back to the room. A band was setting up in the corner. The drums were up and the microphones were turned on. The three men settled in to play, and she listened to their mellow music with pleasure as her drink was served.

She barely noticed that a new musician had joined the trio. With a double take, she saw that the man with the saxophone was none other than Luke! Dressed in black chinos and a slate-grey silk shirt open at the collar, he looked mysterious . . . dangerous.

Boldly taking his stance in front of the guitar player, he brought the saxophone to his lips and blew a long, flowing note that took flight and soared with grace, as the piano, guitar, and drums accompanied him.

The wine was beginning to soften the edges of the day, and Catlin allowed the song to wash over her. He was good. Very good. She wasn't even sure he'd seen her, until his eyes locked onto hers as he moved his hips in rhythm to the music. Each note was a call, beckoning her to join him in his dance. The room grew warmer and Catlin felt a sheen of perspiration form on her neck. Her body swayed, the motion almost involuntary.

Luke moved from the bandstand toward her, still playing. Nothing else in the room was visible as he approached. The tension in her body was mounting with each step he took. Only three more paces and he would be with her. . . .

When he stopped, Catlin half-rose to greet him. His eyes didn't let go, but she felt the room around her for the first time since he'd begun to play. Averting her glance, she shifted self-consciously, aware of the other people in the bar staring at her.

Mike Graham, an assistant cameraman she'd met earlier that day, walked toward her. He carried a martini glass in one hand and a jar of olives in the other. It was clear he intended to join her for the duration of the evening. Luke had gone back to the bandstand, but continued to watch her.

"Hi, Catlin," Mike said, sitting down across the

table from her. He sipped his martini and popped an olive into his mouth. "How's it shakin'?"

"Everything's swell. How's by you?"

"All under control," he said with a wink. "Got some great stuff today. Some of your suggestions were really useful. That over-the-shoulder shot of the slaves was particularly. . . ."

His words drifted away as she connected again with Luke. His eyes drew her away from the table, away from the realities of the bar, and the unwelcome attention of her guest. Placing the saxophone on his lips, he paused for a moment, and she waited breathlessly for the note that was about to come.

Once again, he enchanted her with his song, each phrase designed to weave a spell of magic around her. Already, the wanting in her body taunted her with a heavy pulsing that had nothing to do with the rhythm of the music. This beat—the throbbing in her breast and the moist apex of her thighs—was the cadence of a much more ancient ritual.

"Well, I'll see ya."

Mike was standing next to her, his jar of olives tucked neatly under his arm, a knowing smile on his lips. She blushed as she realized he had witnessed her reaction to Luke and his music.

"Oh, jeez, Mike. I'm sorry. I. . . ."

The cameraman glanced at Luke and gave him a salute. Turning back, he took her hand in his. "If the music man turns out to be less than perfect, you know where I'm staying."

Her blush deepened as he sauntered back to his table. Turning her attention once again to Luke, she stared at the man who could capture her with a glance. He had rolled his long sleeves up and his strong arms held his instrument like a lover. His muscles tensed as he played a scale. She couldn't help but wonder what it would be like to be held by those steely arms, to have those hands explore her body.

Leaving the bandstand again, Luke moved toward her. He was playing an old Billie Holliday song that she loved. Feet apart, knees slightly bent, he stood in front of her and let the music speak for him. The tension she felt was becoming unbearable. Grasping her wine glass, she drank deeply and the tart liquid flowed through her body like hot spice.

The song ended, and he meandered back to the stage. There was something very unnerving about this unexplainable, intoxicating excitement she felt as she watched him. She prided herself on controlling her emotions, not letting anyone get the better of her good judgment. Listening to the passionate messages Luke was sending through his music, his body, and his mesmerizing eyes, she felt on the brink of giving herself to him . . . relinquishing logic, discretion, and caution.

Shaking her head, she tried to clear her thoughts, to get a grip on her untrustworthy emotions. What was he doing to her? Had he slipped a magic potion into her drink? How could a man she barely knew affect her this deeply?

Scrambling for the check and her purse, Catlin knew she had to make a run for it. It was far too dangerous to stay under the influence of the special effects man. She couldn't look at him. Not even for a second.

Luke placed his sax in the stand next to the piano. Never had his music meant more. The instrument had become a part of him, the part that could speak more eloquently than he'd ever dared. And she'd responded. He could see from her eyes, from the flush on her soft cheeks, that his message was getting through.

Turning back toward the audience, he stopped dead in his tracks. Catlin was gone. He searched the room frantically, peering into the dark corners to no avail. Walking stiffly to her table, he saw the neat stack of bills laid there to pay her tab. She was really gone. He turned to leave, but the waitress stopped him. She handed him a folded napkin. "The lady asked me to give this to you."

"Thank you." He handed the woman a dollar bill, then turned his attention to the napkin.

"You play wonderfully. But the only song I can hear now is 'On My Own.' Catlin."

Folding the note, Luke shook his head, then put the paper in his pocket. She was quite a puzzle. Hot, cold; yes, no, maybe. All in one day. But if he had anything to do with it, by this time next week, he'd be playing "The Look of Love."

Catlin was the first person in the mini-van. Although it was only five a.m., six other sleepy crew members climbed in and filled the rest of the seats. She didn't turn her head to look for Luke's truck, but she had a sneaking suspicion that if it wasn't there, it soon would be.

"What are you doing up so early?" Sylvia plopped herself in the seat next to Catlin. "Don't you know one of the perks of being associate producer is that you don't have to report 'till last crew call?"

"There's no rest for the wicked." Catlin smiled,

hoping the wardrobe woman wouldn't press her for a more reasonable answer.

"You haven't been here long enough to be wicked. And once you *are* wicked, you sure won't be getting up at five."

"Sylvia," said Catlin, as if she were scandalized. "How can you even think that I'm here to do anything but work?"

"Because you're young and gorgeous, that's how. And then, there's Luke."

"We're just friends."

Sylvia laughed. "You're gonna have to be more original than that." Her grin changed from mischievous to sincere. "Listen, honey. There's only one guy on this whole motley crew that I give a hoot about, and that's Luke McKeever. If I were a few years younger, I'd give you a run for your money."

"There'd be no competition. Besides, Luke is very nice, but I meant that about us being friends."

Sylvia patted her on the hand. "Okay, dear. Have it your own way. But mark my words, you two have more than friendship brewing. Just be careful, honey, and know what you're getting into. But what the hell. Enjoy him while you can."

The van came to a stop before Catlin could think of a suitable reply. After Sylvia and the rest of the crew got off, Catlin sat staring at nothing, thinking about what the older woman had said.

Were her feelings for Luke so obvious that everyone could see right through her? Did *he* know how he'd gotten under her skin, how it was a constant battle to hide the wanting? Was she destined to fall in love and, once again, be hurt so badly she'd want to die? After all, even Sylvia knew it would all be temporary.

"You want to go back to the motel, little lady?"

She looked up to see the driver patiently waiting for her to make a move. "No, I'll get off. Sorry."

The early morning air was chilly, so she made her way over to the catering truck for a warming cup of coffee. The key grip was standing in front of her, his arm casually slung around the waist of the prop lady. Her head rested against his shoulder, and they were talking so softly that Catlin couldn't make out the words.

She wondered when they had met, what had happened to bring these two people together. Was the prop woman feeling about her beau the way she was feeling about Luke? Or were they both veterans, used to loving a little, and leaving a lot?

"There you are."

Catlin froze. It was Luke. Her stomach tightened, but it wasn't fear or tension making the knots. It was excitement. This must be what they meant by heart flutters, she thought, because there was a rapid quivering in her chest that grew stronger as she turned to face him.

"I looked for you this morning, but you'd run off."

His silver T-shirt clung to his chest, outlining muscles that begged to be touched. His belt buckle was copper, and below that she couldn't stop herself from noticing that his jeans were button-fly, not zippered. Catlin felt her face flush as she tore her gaze away from his pants and looked at his face.

Big mistake. For she was captured instantly by his startling blue eyes, and they held her as securely as a flame holds a moth. "What . . . why . . . what are you doing here so early?"

"I have to get Harriet ready for her scene," he said. "She's in the first shot this morning, so I want to explain to her what she's got to do."

"Explain?"

"Well, yeah. She's got to prepare, you know. Get motivated."

He wasn't smiling. She honestly couldn't tell if he was kidding or not. The safest thing to do was nod.

"Come with me. She likes you. I'm sure she wouldn't mind."

"I'm deeply honored."

Luke ordered two cups of coffee, then took the steaming brew to the condiment table. "Donut?"

She shook her head and took her cup.

"Well?" He looked at her expectantly.

She really didn't have anything terribly pressing to do for at least an hour. And she was very curious as to how one goes about motivating a pig. "Okay," she said with a sigh. She'd be strong later. "Lead on."

Catlin was silent as they walked across the lawn toward the big truck. There was so much confusion in her mind. Each time she swore she wasn't going to get involved with Luke, she turned right around and jumped in with both feet. Her head was saying one thing, and her heart just the opposite. What troubled her was that, for the first time in her life, she was completely willing to disregard her common sense. It was the scariest, most exciting thing she'd ever done.

"Here, sweetie. Harriet."

Luke barely got the words out of his mouth before

the pig ran out of the doghouse and into his arms. Harriet was so excited, she wiggled all over. Catlin knew just how she felt.

"There's my girl." Luke stroked and petted the tiny animal, who grunted very daintily in return. "Here's your breakfast, girl." He walked over to the truck and pulled out a bag of unidentifiable foodstuff and poured it into the dog . . . pig bowl. Harriet made short work of her meal, then turned back to her master, who picked her up and cradled her like a baby.

"I can't get over this. She's such a . . . unique pet."

"Yeah," he said, proud as a peacock. He turned his head and stared straight at Catlin. "She's one of a kind."

She was standing two feet away from the man, but he held her frozen with his gaze. It was as if the space in front of her evaporated until all that was in her field of vision was his face. She wanted to touch his freshly shaven cheek, to run her tongue over his lips and taste him. More than anything, she wanted to be in his arms.

"Cat . . ." He put his pet on the ground and then he was next to her . . . too close.

She closed her eyes as he touched her lips with his fingertips. Her knees grew shaky as the back of his hand brushed the side of her face so gently that it was like being kissed by a butterfly. She had to step back before she fell into his arms.

But what she fell over was Harriet. She moved away and felt the tiny pig knock into her ankle. "Oh, help, wait." She stumbled backwards, lifting her feet high to avoid stepping on Harriet. Luke was trying to catch her, and then he was tripping over the pig. Catlin sat down, right in the middle of the mud puddle. Luke landed on top of her, his arms straddling her chest, his legs stretched out behind him. Harriet watched.

"I guess she's motivated," Luke said dryly.

When Catlin peeked under Luke's arm and looked at Harriet, she could have sworn the swine was smiling.

By the time lunch was called, Catlin had marked off four scenes as completed and had finished making all the script changes for the day. She'd missed Harriet's screen debut. After scrounging up a pair of slacks from the wardrobe trailer, she'd felt too foolish to go and see Luke and his stunt pig. Actually, she'd figured it was God's way of telling her to keep her distance from both man and beast.

Folding her script, she turned to walk to the lunch truck when she saw him making his way toward her. Her heart skipped a beat and the warning light went off in her head.

"Cat," he said, looking at her warily. "Everything okay?"

"Yeah. I enjoy a good swim before work. So, how did she do?"

"She was excellent. No pig in the world could've done the scene more convincingly. And in only one take."

"You must be proud."

He just beamed.

She gave up. She just couldn't stay wary of this loony guy. He was so crazy about that pig. Maybe he was just crazy. But, what the heck. She would let herself enjoy him and how he made her heart feel light. For now.

As they walked toward the catering truck, she saw that most of the crew was gathered in groups, busily talking away. "It's nice that they all know each other." she said.

"A lot of us have worked together before. Hollywood's such a small town that those of us who do distant locations inevitably run into each other again and again. I've worked with Vogel on three pictures. He hires the same production manager, who hires the crew. We've become like family on these movies. The funny thing is, I rarely see any of them when I'm at home. I like them a lot, but my other life seems separate, somehow."

They reached the open window of the catering truck and a sweating, beefy man pointed a ladle at Catlin. "What you want?" he asked with a distinct Italian accent.

"What you got?" she shot back.

"Lasagna, roast beef, trout. Vegetables, rice, potatoes. Pick what you want, but be fast, eh?" He gestured toward the long line behind her.

"Trout, rice, vegetables, okay?"

"Good choice. You like."

He handed her a plate filled with a whole trout, a very large portion of rice, and a heaping, steaming spoon of broccoli. She would never be able to eat it all. She wanted to give some of it back, but the cook was already doling out someone else's food, and he paid no attention to her. Luke's plate was equally filled, so she gave up and they went to sit at one of the long tables.

"You'll appreciate the portions as the days get longer," Luke said.

"This is enough food for a week!"

"Then you aren't working hard enough. I'll have to figure out a way for you to burn more calories." He smiled at her mischievously. "One thing comes to mind. . . ."

She felt herself blushing. She was mostly embarrassed because she'd thought of that herself.

"You could help me load rifles. That works up a sweat in no time."

She jerked around to look at his face. He seemed serious, with no trace of a grin. He hadn't been talking about rifles, she was sure, but when he looked at her, his face was innocence itself.

"Speaking of loading rifles, have you given anymore thought to bumping up my budget?"

She grinned. He was nothing if not persistent. "Yes," she said. "I have. I'll give you a thousand, but that's it."

"A thousand?" He thought for a moment. "Cool. That's a real good start."

"I'm not kidding, Luke. That's all I can give you. Make it last."

He took her hand in his and kissed it with a great flourish. "You are the best. I knew I could count on you."

She took her hand back, flustered that his kiss had made her quiver. "The only reason I can give you anything is because we re-cast the role of Edward and the new actor was a lot cheaper. If that hadn't happened. . . ."

"I know. and I'm grateful. Now, finish up," he said. "I want to take a walk before lunch is over."

Catlin sighed and continued eating the enormous meal. She managed to get half of it down, then pushed the plate away.

"That's it. I can't eat another bite."

"Great. Let's go." Luke took her plate with his, and dumped them both in the trash. He took her arm and led her away from the crew. "I want to show you something. I found it last week."

She stalled. "This 'something' doesn't have four legs, does it?"

"No," he said, laughing. "This is mineral, not animal or vegetable."

They walked past the trailers and trucks until they reached a long fence with a hinged gate. He swung the gate open and took her hand to lead her. She welcomed his touch and explored his large palm with her thumb. As he picked up the pace, his whole demeanor spoke of adventure. She was swept up in his excitement as they wandered into a forest of pecan trees so dense the sunlight could only come through in dappled streams.

The ground was soft and crunched as she stepped on twigs and dried leaves. The air was thick with a musty odor, like the inside of an old bookshop. There was no path, but Luke walked purposefully along, turning at an old dead tree stump and winding through the hanging branches.

He stopped, stood behind her, and put his hands over her eyes. "I don't want you to peek," he whispered. He took a step forward, and pressed his body against the back of hers. She was completely enfolded by his arms and hands. She was disconcerted for a second, but that passed as she grew accustomed to his nearness.

The smell of the woods mingled with his unique scent, and she breathed deeply, enjoying the use of her other senses. She heard his breath, even and deep, next to her ear. Every part of her body sang with contentment as they continued walking.

Luke stopped. They stood completely still for a moment. She could feel his breath quicken on the back of her neck. A soft moan escaped his lips. Without moving his hands, he kissed her lightly on the shoulder—the softest, most electrifying touch in the world.

Her legs felt weak and she tried to hold on to something, but there was nothing in front of her. Luke took his hands away from her face, and she saw his discovery.

Directly in front of her, in a soft golden glade, was a wishing well. It was obviously very old. The stones were worn and chipped, the crank was broken off and weeds had climbed the sides. Light streamed down into the well, carrying particles of glitter into its hidden depths.

"Oh, Luke, it's beautiful!" She ran to the well and leaned over the side. Peering into the black hole, she laughed with wonder. The forest was filled with the sound of her voice, each echo a declaration of her delight.

Luke joined her. "I'm so glad you like it. It makes me think of you—a treasure I didn't expect to find."

"Oh my," Catlin said, as a shiver ran along her spine. He certainly knew the right things to say. She took a deep breath and turned her attention to the well. "I have to make a wish." She dug into her pocket and pulled out a shiny copper penny. Closing her eyes tightly, she tossed the coin, wishing with all her heart that the beautiful dream she was in would go on and on.

Luke's coin followed, and then he was next to her. She looked into his eyes, and before she could speak his name, his lips were crushing hers. She closed her eyes and melted next to Luke's chest, wrapping her arms around his broad shoulders, feeling his muscles tense as he moved even closer against her. His tongue parted her teeth and tentatively explored her mouth.

She quivered with such a strong yearning for him that she was frightened of the power of her emotions. Her head whirled with thoughts and sensations she had never experienced before. She wanted him, not just his lips, but all of him. She wanted. . . .

She jerked herself away. "Wait. This wasn't supposed to happen."

He stared at her for a long moment. "Okay, Cat," he whispered softly. "This whole thing has sort of taken me by surprise. I just want you so badly."

She turned from him, leaving the hard wall of his chest, the safe haven of his arms. She couldn't look at his penetrating eyes and his soft mouth. Everything about Luke was tempting, and she didn't need that in her life.

"It's time we went back," she said, wishing now that things were different, that she didn't know better than to get mixed up with someone like Luke. But she knew from experience that wishes seldom come true.

Gently, he took her hand and led her through the woods. She wasn't thinking clearly. Their entwined fingers were the only tangible remains of the kiss that still sensitized her lips. Where was her self-control?

She *had* to concentrate on work. She couldn't afford an affair with a crew member. She didn't want any kind of affair at all! And then she looked at his face, the shadows of the trees playing over his eyes. Her resolve began to weaken, but then the warning voice in her head said stop—he's not for you.

They hurried back. Catlin was glad because she needed to be on safer ground. The thought of his kiss, how he had held her with an urgency she found herself mirroring, was terribly unsettling. The crew was returning to work just as they closed the wooden gate behind them. Luke squeezed her hand when they reached his truck. "I'll give you a ride home after we wrap. I want to take you to dinner tonight."

"I don't think so. Not tonight. You know, work . . . And thanks, Luke. I'll never forget the wishing well."

"I'm glad," he said, looking deep into her eyes. "But don't count out tonight. Let's just see what happens." He bent closer to her, as if he intended to kiss her again. Instead, he said, "By the way, my wish came true." He left her standing next to his unsightly truck.

All the strange and scary feelings still lingered in her heart, but his words brought a smile to her lips. What she needed was a moment to adjust to the real world.

She walked over to the honey-wagon, and locked herself into a compartment. The room was so tiny that she could barley turn around, but it was private and that was what she needed. Catlin stood in front of the mirror, amazed that the woman looking back at her was so easily swayed by a soft word and a gentle touch. She shook her head, fluffed her hair, and reapplied her lipstick.

She had to be professional while she was at work, she thought. Maybe having dinner with Luke wasn't such a great idea. On the other hand, it was a fine way to test her mettle. Would she be able to keep her promise to herself, and insist that they just be friends?

Catlin took a long, hard look at the face in the mirror. *Get a grip on yourself, girl. It's all going to be over soon, and you're going to say good-bye to Luke McKeever, forever. Don't get in over your head.*

With new resolve, she unlocked the door and returned to her place beside the camera. It took every inch of self-control, but she was determined to be the picture of professionalism for the rest of the day . . . and with luck, the rest of the shoot.

FOUR

The catfish swam in the tank—ugly, whiskered, and staring straight at her. The fish was oblivious to the fact that she would soon be having it as a main course. An involuntary shudder jerked Catlin's shoulder away from the protective arm of her date.

"Is something wrong?" Luke asked.

"No, nothing." The smile she offered him was weaker than she'd intended. She turned so that her back was to the tank.

"This is such an interesting restaurant. How did you find it?" The cheeriness of her voice sounded phony, but she decided that with a big enough smile, he wouldn't catch on.

He didn't.

"I heard about it from the locals. You can't get fresher catfish. And the cornbread is made with hot peppers. Never tasted anything like it. You'll love it."

"Uh huh." The smile was starting to hurt.

The white, off-the-shoulder dress she'd worn for their first evening out seemed a poor choice now. Everyone in the crowded restaurant was wearing casual clothing: shorts, jeans, T-shirts. Luke was dressed in black slacks, a purple shirt, and cowboy boots. As she studied his tall, muscular body, her false smile became genuine and warm. She recalled the pleasure so evident on his face when he'd picked her up this evening. On second thought, the dress *was* a good choice.

He reached a hand toward her, and she extended her own. Their eyes met as he took a step nearer, and she was impressed once again by the clear blue intensity in his. Neither of them spoke. Surprisingly, she felt no need to fill in the silence with idle conversation.

They were finally seated at a long picnic table across from a family from Des Moines. Their name tags said so. Bill and Darlene were dressed in matching jeans and windbreakers, with T-shirts that had large red arrows pointing to each other topped by block letters stating I'M WITH THE JERK. The children, twin boys of about seven, were socking each other back and forth on the shoulder. Each punch was accompanied by a loud ouch. Bill and Darlene ignored them.

On Catlin's right, a small, gray-haired man with coke-bottle-thick glasses glared at the children. She could hear him muttering under his breath, but couldn't make out the words.

She turned her attention to Luke. "Where are the menus?

"No menus. It's *prix fixe*. Just sit back and relax. The food will be here in a minute."

He was positively glowing. The punching bags across the way didn't seem to faze him at all. As a matter-of-fact, he looked like the cat who ate the canary. Was it because she'd agreed to go out with him? If he thought this meant any more than a friendly dinner, she'd just have to tell him it didn't. If only there was a quiet, private place to talk.

Reaching over the plastic salt and pepper shakers, Luke grabbed a tin bucket and placed it in front of her. Inside the bucket were silverware and paper napkins.

"Oh, look," she said. "I found a fork with only one bent tine. And this one's dirty, but it's straight as an arrow."

"A little dirt never hurt anyone," he said. He took the dirty fork and wiped it on a napkin. "Take a look at those kids. Aren't they great?" The two boys had escalated their warfare, which now included pinching as well as poking.

"Charming." She wondered about her judgment as she glanced around the room. Everyone was eating and laughing, enjoying the atmosphere. Maybe she was being too harsh. Luke certainly seemed to be having a good time. And if he thought those kids were great, he would be crazy about the waitress.

She was dressed in a red-and-white checked uniform with layers of white petticoats raising her skirt to waist level. She brought platters of food to the table.

"Hey, how you doin'? My name's Esther Louise and I'll be servin' y'all tonight. You need any little thing, you jes holler."

She carried a mound of catfish, heads still attached, eyes bulging, and dumped them directly in front of

Catlin. In front of Luke, a huge silver platter of steaming greens was dropped from about five inches above the table. The juice showered the immediate area, including his shirt. He smiled. It seemed to be the highlight of his dining experience.

Baskets of cornbread, buckets of whipped butter, and thick, deep-fried onion rings covered the rest of the table. Enormous beer steins were handed to each adult, and smaller versions, containing milk, were given to the twins.

"Eat up. This stuff is truly great. You could never get this in LA . . . and the atmosphere . . . real Southern country." He placed a whole catfish on her tin plate.

The fish stared at her. Neither of them blinked. She picked up her fork and gingerly took a small helping of greens. She almost made it all the way to her mouth. Putting her full fork back down, she turned the fish so that he was staring at Darlene. She pushed some greens over the catfish and took a large bite of cornbread.

Turning to Luke with a smile and a nod, she felt pleased that she was managing the situation. Then the fire started. Her mouth was ablaze with jalapeno! Eyes watering, she grabbed her beer stein and gulped the cold liquid down.

It didn't help.

She paused for a gasp, then downed the rest of the beer. Finally, she could feel the fire subside. She heard Luke's laughter.

She turned to him with what she hoped was a deadly glare. "We'll have to come here often," she said.

"Oh, God," he said, wiping his eyes. "I

shouldn't be laughing. Really, I feel awful about this. I tried to warn you about the cornbread. Tell you what. To make up for it, I'll take you to Bojangles after dinner. How does champagne, soft music, and a quiet table sound?''

"All right for starters. But the champagne better be imported."

Luke took another bite of fish. It was cooked to perfection. Everything about this evening was perfect. Especially Catlin. She looked so beautiful in white. It set off her dark hair and made her skin glow. He watched her take a tiny bite of fish. Her femininity and grace had attracted him from the start. And on top of all that, she was damn good at her job, although a little too tight with a buck.

"So, how do you like Natchez?" he asked.

"All I've seen are Tearose, the hotel, and the Piggly Wiggly. Not much by which to judge."

"Don't worry, I'll show you all the best places. This one was just the beginning."

"Wonderful." Catlin groaned inwardly. If this was the beginning, she didn't want to be around for the end. This place was definitely not her style. L'Orangerie. That was for her. And yet, she did still want to be friends with Luke. Maybe they could just stay at the motel from now on. No, that would be awkward. She would just have to find a nice place for them to go. One with private tables and maybe even a menu.

Dinner finally ended with only a minor skirmish over who would pay the check. Luke outweighed her by a good eighty pounds, so he won.

They left the restaurant and walked in the warm evening air, underneath a canopy of willow trees.

Luke pointed out the nearby dock where the *Delta Queen*, a huge paddle wheel boat that was now a pleasure cruise ship, was anchored. The lapping water of the Mississippi was a gentle reminder that she was far from home.

Ever since she'd been a child, she'd wanted to see the mighty river. And now, as they walked slowly in the warm sultry evening, she felt as if she were in a storybook—with Luke as her dashing hero.

They made their way to Bojangles, enjoying the stillness of the night. He opened a solid oak door for her, and they entered another world.

A band played softly in the dimly lit room. Beautifully dressed couples, swaying to the music, flowed across the dance floor. Plush carpeting covered the seating area and elegantly framed prints dotted the walls. The bar covered the entire west wall, and the bartender looked cosmopolitan in his white shirt and black bow tie. The waiters wore tuxedos, and not one of them looked as if he would want her to holler.

They were seated at a private table and the champagne was brought out quickly. After pouring each of them a glass, the waiter left, without introducing himself.

Luke picked up his glass and held it toward her. "To you, Cat, and all the adventures we're going to have." He drank deeply as she sipped and thought about his words.

Did she want adventures with him? After that dinner, he was on shaky ground, but his choice of nightspots was quickly improving his overall average. Maybe an adventure was just what she needed. She gestured for another toast. "To distant locations. A brief, magical time where real life fades into the background.'' She finished her drink and stood up. "All right, twinkle-toes. Let's go."

She led him to the dance floor. The burnished wood platform reflected lights from the kaleidoscope of colors that flickered from an overhead glass ball. The band played soft dance music from the forties that conjured up images of Fred and Ginger dancing cheek to cheek.

With a grace that took her breath away, he took her in his arms. Just the feel of his hand touching her back made her stomach do a dance of its very own. She was held firmly as he arched her back and brought his lips so near that they almost kissed. She breathed deeply, captivated by his scent.

Then, he proceeded to sweep her off her feet.

He danced like a dream. She was close to him . . . close enough to feel his chest expand, his muscles contract, his heart beat. They moved as one on the dance floor. Each step flowed into another as she let him lead her. The more she relaxed, the more prophetic she became, knowing an instant before that he would turn, glide, sway.

There was no space between them. Catlin rested her head on Luke's shoulder and felt his strength. It aroused her, as did the dance. Acutely aware of her body against his, she knew that he felt her excitement. He was responding in kind. The heat of his loins penetrated her dress, and she was overwhelmed by a longing she didn't want to recognize.

The music stopped, ending their closeness before she was ready. She looked up to meet his gaze. The intensity of his desire shocked her, and she stepped back, closing her eyes.

"I need some champagne." Her voice was husky. She opened her eyes, and saw that he, too, was unsteady.

"To say the least." The strain in his voice was obvious. They walked off the dance floor, not touching.

"My, oh my, that was some dance. Why didn't you tell me you were really Gene Kelly?" They reached the table and he held her chair.

"I don't tell all my secrets. There are lots of things you're just going to have to discover along the way." He sat down and took her hand. "You weren't so bad yourself."

"Aw, shucks." She turned her head demurely. "You say that to all the girls."

"No, as a matter-of-fact, I don't. I like it that we dance well together. That's important to me."

Yes, she could see that it was something that would matter to him. Since she'd met him, it had been obvious that he cared deeply about his work and his music. His enthusiasm was contagious, and the urge to know more about him was strong. She settled into her seat more comfortably, but never took her eyes from him. "What else is important to you?" she asked, trying to regain her equilibrium. It was difficult when he looked at her that way.

After a sip of champagne, Luke stared at his hands for a moment. When he brought his eyes up to meet hers, she saw such a clarity of purpose shining from them that she listened as if it were the most important thing she would ever hear.

"My work," he said. "I love what I do, and I do it well. That's not ego, it's just fact. I like the travel, the challenge. My family . . . my uncle taught me the business and he was the best." He paused again, but this time he didn't take a drink, he just moved forward in his seat. "And you."

His eyes said more than his words. He wanted her, and God help her, she wanted him. She knew that their beginning would be wonderful. He awakened a raw need in her that had been dormant for too long. But the end . . . it would kill her.

After a deep breath, she made her decision.

"What's important to me is my job. I'm going to be a producer. That's all that counts to me now. I have no time for anything else." She stood, almost tipping her chair over. "Excuse me." She walked briskly to the ladies' room.

What was she doing? she asked herself. Alone in the lounge, she stared at her reflection in the mirror, searching her face for an answer. This relationship was crazy. She had to put a stop to it right now. It wasn't fair to him, or to herself. Luke should find someone else to play house with. She didn't participate in that game any more. Not now. Not ever.

She shook her head. As attracted as she was, she could see no way to come out of a relationship with Luke intact. Unless she put on the brakes tonight, someone was going to be hurt . . . and it was no secret who that someone would be.

Squaring her shoulders, she turned from the mirror and walked back to join him. He was standing, his back straight and stiff, next to the table. The room seemed chilly and dark as she neared him.

The band played a slow, sad song with such melancholy that her throat tightened. As she reached her chair, he turned to look at her. She'd made her choice too late—and the wrong person had been wounded. She could see the sadness in Luke's eyes, the confusion on his brow.

That couldn't be helped. The situation would be a lot worse if she let it continue. "It's late," she said, her voice strained. "I need to be getting back."

He took a drink and turned away. "Right." He paid the bill, and they left. This time, when they walked under the gently swaying branches of the willow trees, she didn't feel their magic, just a sadness that gripped her heart like a tight fist.

When he opened the truck door for her, Catlin got in quickly, averting her gaze so she wouldn't have to face him. She sat close to the door, as close as her body could squeeze. The cold metal of the handle hurt as it pressed into her side. But she was still too close. She could feel him next to her; the very air was charged with his presence.

The once beautiful evening had lost all of its charm, and she wanted desperately to be alone in her motel room. He started the engine and the noise was magnified in the quiet of the cab.

It wasn't a long trip, but she felt as if each street had a stoplight and each one was red. The words that had hurt him replayed over and over in her head, and grew more severe and uncaring as they drove on in the awkward stillness.

They turned the final corner, and Catlin forced herself to look at his reflection in the front window. The harsh planes of his face had unnatural shadows where the lights from the street seemed to cut him. His jaw was clenched and a small muscle moved once, just below his right eye. His pain was her pain; it couldn't be ignored or denied. A quiet realization came to her as she studied his sad, luminous eyes.

"I need you, Luke," she said softly, not daring to glance at him. "I need you to be my friend. I just can't get serious now. You're the nicest person I've met in a very long time, and I want to be able to see you. I don't have any other friends here."

He pulled into the parking lot and stopped the pickup before he spoke. His silence drew her, his smile was sad and sweet. Catlin was afraid of what she'd see lurking in the azure shadows of his eyes. But his defenses were intact. Instead of his soul, she saw twin reflections of herself. "I give you my word. You won't get any pressure from me. We'll just be friends. How's that?"

She felt her shoulders relax as she smiled in return. "Great." She leaned over to kiss his cheek, but he turned suddenly, and she found herself kissing him on the lips. The velvet shock of his mouth on hers sent an urgent message through her body. His lips demanded her true feelings, and she couldn't deny that she wanted him. He pulled her closer, until her body was pressed up against him . . . and the kiss never stopped.

Luke explored her mouth with his tongue, setting her aflame. His hands, nestled in the small of her back, brought her so near him that she could feel the muscles of his chest. Their skin seemed to thin and merge until they blended together as one being.

Catlin's heart pounded, and she knew he felt her excitement. The dress she wore didn't conceal the hardness of her nipples as she rubbed against him. The fire that consumed her was almost out of control.

No, she thought, this isn't fair. This wasn't part of the deal. She fought him; fought to be released from the spell he was casting. She pushed against his chest. He didn't resist. "I have to go," she whispered.

She left him in the truck and ran to her room.

The next morning, Luke drove to the front of the motel to pick Catlin up. She wasn't there. He wondered if she'd left early just to avoid him. Disappointed, he drove to work, thinking about the evening they had spent together.

Why couldn't he let this relationship idea drop? Be friends, just like she wanted? What was it about Catlin Clark that made him so determined to have her?

The crazy thing was, she was all wrong for him. She'd said it herself—her job came first. And a woman who was that set on getting ahead was exactly the type he'd sworn to avoid.

Hadn't he learned anything from his divorce? Susan had been a career woman, and that's all she'd been. Marriage had always come second in her book, and that eventually had been their undoing. His being on the road hadn't helped, but she'd made it perfectly clear that what she needed was a man to climb with her up the ladder of success. A special effects man didn't cut it.

Dammit, he'd tried. He'd gone with her to the endless, boring business dinners, but he'd known she was embarrassed by him. He wasn't suit-and-tie enough for her. Now she had herself a nice corporate attorney. They could snuggle up to their briefcases together and have a merry old time.

Was Catlin so very different? She loved her work and was already entrenched in the corporate side of the business. She'd probably be a line producer soon, and then what would she want with a working-class guy like him? Would it matter that he was considered to be one of the best in the business?

And yet. . . .

In a lot of ways she was the opposite of his ex-wife. Catlin loved the movie business, didn't she? And he'd seen how much she wanted to be with him. It was in her eyes, in her kiss. Surely, she could see the advantages of a short-term relationship. No strings attached, no time for things to get ugly. He was just taking things too fast, that's all.

The loneliness of the road was getting to him, causing him to reach out and grab that which could only be given. She couldn't be rushed, and pulling her close would only make her push away. He would have to take a different tack. If that didn't work, then he'd just be her friend. But, oh, what a waste that would be. They were meant to be more . . . much more.

He pulled in to his parking spot next to Bessie. Only a few people milled around the catering truck. He didn't want coffee. Harriet needed feeding and there was that hole in the chicken wire fence around her pen he had to fix. That should keep him occupied for awhile. He jumped onto the tailgate, and walked through his truck without noticing anything. But when he got to the back door, he heard a sound he shouldn't have . . . a human voice.

He swung the door open, ready for a fight. Let anyone touch one hair of that pig's head and he'd. . . .

"Hi."

Luke released the air he'd been holding and relaxed his tensed muscles. Brandon. The boy was sitting cross-legged on the ground next to Harriet's house. The pig was nuzzling his hand, anxious to be petted. "What are you doing in here?" Luke asked.

"Pettin' the pig. You said I could. I 'member. We was standing right over there." He nodded his head in the general direction of the two-acre lawn. "It's okay, ain't it?"

Luke nodded. "Next time, ask. I don't like the idea of you being here by yourself." He walked down the steps and sat next to the boy. "Something might happen to Harriet."

Brandon shrugged away the hand that tousled his hair, but he grinned happily. Then his attention went back to Harriet. He was entranced with the pig. While his eyes danced watching her sniff and grunt and wiggle, he whispered quiet words of affection, words he probably didn't realize he was saying. "Yeah, that's it. Come on, baby. You like that? I love you, too."

Luke sighed. Sometimes he thought about having a kid of his own. A kid like Brandon. His son would have dark hair, of course, and be just a bit bigger. But he'd be curious and daring, just like this one. The things he would teach his son. The ball games they'd go to. The places they'd travel to. And the mother they'd both love.

Catlin.

Now, where the hell had that thought come from? He wasn't ready for marriage or a commitment, not with Catlin, not with anybody. Sure, maybe someday he'd have a family, but that would come later . . . much later. Now, he had work to do.

Catlin thought about the previous evening while she sipped her coffee. She'd found a director's chair near the catering truck and was content to sit and wait for the rest of the crew to arrive. She was more confused about her feelings than she cared to admit. Everything seemed so simple when she was away from Luke. She could see her path and knew each step she had to take to get to the top. The path was only wide enough for one.

Much as she hated to admit it, Luke's job didn't help matters either. Hollywood had a very distinct class system and it was difficult to break the mold. She'd always thought of herself as someone who would never let anything such as appearances bother her. So the niggling thoughts about how their relationship would look were quickly pushed to the back of her mind. No, the real problem was about loving *anyone*, not just the special effects man.

Catlin knew the compromises that went along with a relationship. His needs had to be met. His schedule had to be considered. Her career would take a backseat and, in this business, that meant failure. She was competing with men. Men who had the little woman at home, supporting them, making them dinners, taking care of the kids, clearing the way for them to put all their energy into winning.

There was no way Luke McKeever was going to make her lose. If she couldn't control her emotions around him, then she wouldn't be around him.

She got herself some more coffee and a breakfast burrito, needing the fuel for the long day ahead. The crew arrived in groups, talking animatedly about the movie, or about their private lives. They were all so comfortable with each other, and she was obviously not a part of their inner circle. Their conversations were easy, like family. Some grips walked by and she said good morning. One man nodded in her direction, the others never even looked up. Being separate was the only part of her job she didn't like. She knew that they regarded her as management with the power to hire and fire. But she missed the camaraderie she'd known before she became an associate producer.

She walked to the production trailer. Work swallowed up the morning, and she didn't come out until almost eleven. By that time, three scenes had been shot and the company was preparing for a move. They were going to shoot the next four scenes a few miles down the road. The hands were busy gathering the equipment that would be needed. Tearose would still be home base, so the big rigs would be left where they were.

A bus was loading and she climbed on board. The crew filled almost every seat, but the only person she saw was Luke. He was sitting by himself in the back. His smile warmed her like the first cup of coffee in the morning.

What the heck, she thought. It's only a five-minute ride. That's what Gilligan thought about a three-hour tour.

She sat next to him anyway.

"Morning," he said. "You left early today. I was going to give you a ride."

"I had a lot of work to do before the move." She didn't look at him. It was a lot safer that way. Even so, she was aware of him. It was as if he were emitting an energy only she could feel. She scooted over a bit closer to the window.

The bus stopped and she made a beeline for the door. They were in a remote area thick with trees. The narrow dirt road where they had parked was filled by the huge trucks of the company, and the crew was busy unloading the equipment for the scene.

She walked over to the director. "Where are we setting up?"

"Come on, I'll show you," Vogel said. "We have to finish this sequence by sunset. I'll want to get a shot at magic hour, and then we can wrap."

They walked deep into the woods. "Magic hour?" she asked.

"That's just before sunset, when the camera picks up soft grays and pinks. It looks magical on the screen."

They reached a small clearing and she saw the camera next to the huge dolly, the machine they used to move the camera over distances without shaking the lens. Next to it was a pile of dolly track that was to be laid down across the clearing. It looked like miniature railroad tracks. She knew it would be a good hour before the camera move was choreographed.

The prop man had just set up behind her. He'd put out director's chairs for the script supervisor, the director, herself, and the actors. She saw Luke put up a leather chair with his name etched on the back. He sat down and sipped a cup of steaming coffee.

"Don't you have work to do?" she asked.

He shook his head. "Nope. No effects today. No one even lights a cigarette. I'm here to watch."

"What about all those guns you have to load?"

"Stan the Man is handling that for me." He smiled in a most beguiling way. "It's great being in charge."

"I see." She turned her attention to the director

once again, acutely aware of the eyes that were watching her every move.

"We got a problem, boss." One of the grips approached Vogel. "The ground is like quicksand. We can't put the dolly down, or it's gonna sink."

"Why didn't someone figure this out before we moved here? Where's the location scout?" Vogel was keeping his temper, barely.

Mike, the cameraman, joined in. "It wasn't like this when we scouted. This must have happened when it rained last week."

Vogel looked at her. "We'll have to move. God knows how long it will take us to find another clearing like this. I need a lot of trees, and enough space to move the camera."

Catlin surveyed the area quickly. There was only about fifty square feet of clearing. "We don't have to move. All we have to do is get boards big enough to disperse the weight."

"They'd have to be very large," said Vogel. "We don't keep those on the truck."

"Luke does," she said. "He's got the walls that we're going to burn next week. You know, the facades."

The group turned to Luke. He was already on his feet.

"You got it. I'll be back in half an hour."

It was only fifteen minutes before he returned with the fake walls. They were placed over the clearing and the dolly track was successfully laid. One hour after they had arrived, they were shooting the first scene.

A cup of coffee was definitely in order, Catlin thought. The coffee table was far too crowded, so she walked slowly toward the prop truck, where she knew there was a small percolator, and some much needed privacy.

"Hey."

She heard Luke's voice and looked around. He was leaning against the camera truck, arms folded across his broad chest.

"Come here."

She walked over to him, studying his arrogant stance and the humor in his eyes.

"That was pretty slick, ace. The brass is gonna be very pleased."

"Just doing my job."

"No. Just doing your job doesn't include creative problem solving. That's extra."

"Thanks." She turned to go, but he caught her shoulder.

"You're special, Cat. You'll make a great producer. And, you're so beautiful it hurts."

His hand burned through the thin material of her shirt. He walked around until he was in front of her, then moved very close. Gently, he stroked her hair, then her cheek. He lifted her chin so he could look into her eyes.

"So beautiful," he whispered. He closed his eyes and kissed her. His lips were soft, the kiss tender.

"Wait." She pulled away from him, angry that he'd broken his word, and even angrier that she was glad. "We're supposed to be friends, remember?"

As she was speaking, Catlin knew the words were a lie, that she wanted him so badly she ached. And, dammit, he kept looking at her with those eyes . . . those eyes that could see far too much.

Then, Luke touched her and her body reacted as

if she had no control. Her arms wrapped around his neck. The rest of the world disappeared until nothing was left but the two of them.

She moaned as he ran his hands down her back. His lips were no longer gentle. Passion made them fierce, desire made them burn. She broke free and gasped.

"Please! Don't do this to me. If you care for me at all, you'll stop. I can't handle this. Not at work. Maybe not at all."

Catlin stepped away and turned her back to him. "I can't be with you now. I'm not very strong, so you'll have to be."

Luke didn't respond. The silence grew, and when she looked for him, he was gone. The emptiness around her was palpable. Never had she felt so alone.

The rest of the day went by in a haze. It was Saturday, and the crew was anxious to be finished. They completed the necessary work and packed up. She hadn't seen Luke since she'd asked him to leave. His chair sat empty until the prop man took it back to his truck.

She was driven back to the motel by the transportation captain. It was dark by the time she arrived. Luke's truck wasn't in the parking lot. Confused and unhappy, she went to her room to write her report for Peters. When the phone rang at nine, she nearly leapt out of her chair. Her heart beat wildly, and then sank when her boss said hello.

Finally finished with her conversation, she looked at the drab, empty room. The walls seemed to close in on her. She grabbed her bag and went down to the bar.

Luke wasn't there. The band that played was one

she hadn't seen before. They played rock and roll, loudly. It should have cheered her when several members of the crew included her in their boisterous conversation. She'd made it; she was accepted now. She'd saved everyone from a grueling day and another company move. It did feel good to be part of the gang, but it didn't stop her heart from aching. She still felt horribly alone. Every time the door opened, Catlin looked for Luke, but he never came. Her laughter felt forced and her mind wandered. Finally, at midnight, she left.

FIVE

The banging on the door wouldn't stop. Catlin pulled the pillow over her ears to shut out the noise, but it didn't help. She opened one eye and peeked at the alarm clock next to her bed. It was eight A.M. Groaning loudly, she thought of several painful ways she could kill whoever had the nerve to be knocking on her door on the only day she was able to sleep in.

The thumping got more insistent, and she crawled out of her warm bed uttering a stream of curses just under her breath. Before she even opened the door, she was yelling at the fool who dared to disturb her. "This better be a matter of life and death, or it's *gonna* be a matter of life and death."

She swung open the door and froze. Luke was leaning against the railing outside her room, smiling easily. Dressed in jeans, a turquoise T-shirt, and cowboy boots, he looked cool and comfortable, far more comfortable than he should have, given the hour. His saxophone case rested next to him. "Morning."

"What are you doing here?"

"Picking you up. We're going exploring." He looked down the length of her body and gave an appreciative nod. "I'm pleased that you're ready to go."

"Oh, God!" The realization that she was dressed in baby-doll pajamas made her cover her most vulnerable areas with her hands, but one look down at her outfit told her she may as well have been naked; the thin material didn't hide a thing.

She slammed the door shut. Her cheeks grew hot enough to start a blaze. "Go away," she yelled.

"Nope." His voice was laced with a maddening amusement.

"I mean it. Go away. I'm not going anywhere with you, Luke McKeever. You're a dangerous man. You surprise people. I hate surprises."

"Face it woman, you're stuck with me. Get dressed. If you're not out here in ten minutes, I'll huff and I'll puff and I'll blow your house down."

Catlin looked at the door. He was out there, and he was going to stay out there until she left the room. She could stay inside until tomorrow morning, but that seemed a bit much. She could get dressed, walk out, and tell him to leave her alone, but that wouldn't put out the fire he'd lit deep within her. Damn him.

Grabbing jeans and a khaki short-sleeved shirt from the closet, she was aware of her rapid heartbeat, and how easily the man flustered her. She quickly brushed her teeth and pulled a comb through her hair.

While she washed her face, it occurred to Catlin that she hadn't put on her boots. So, she took off her jeans, climbed into the boots, and yanked on the jeans once again. She was ready, and it had only taken four minutes. Staring at the clock, she waited until eleven minutes had passed, then opened the door, sure she was making a huge mistake.

"Where are we going?" she asked, as they walked to the car.

"Louisiana. Bayou country. The Great Outdoors. Exploring."

"In other words, you don't know."

"Correct. And we can't be late." He helped her into the truck and jogged around to the driver's seat. Then they were off, heading southeast, to parts unknown.

They drove past the familiar landmarks of downtown Natchez and headed for the highway. "I can't explore anything until I've had coffee." Catlin looked at Luke with what she hoped was an appealing, poignant gaze.

"Can't you wait until we've left Natchez?"

So much for poignant looks. "No. I need caffeine, and I need it quickly."

He sighed dramatically. "Okay."

They pulled into a small coffee shop. The diner was empty, except for one customer who was dressed in a gaudy, flowered housecoat and had tight pink curlers in her hair, at the counter. On her feet were white bunny slippers.

Luke put his arm casually around Catlin's shoulder and whispered, "Maybe someday you'll dress like that for me."

"Hush," she said, as she poked him in the ribs. They settled in a booth next to the window and scanned the plastic menus. Her stomach was starting to let her know coffee wasn't enough. "Have you noticed that everything down here seems to be fried? The only fresh vegetables I've eaten have come from our catering truck."

"I know," he said. "I've tried to convince the chef at the hotel that he doesn't need to fry my eggs in two cups of lard, but he doesn't get the picture. I've been ordering poached eggs, and I don't like poached eggs."

The waitress appeared from the kitchen. Her hair was done in the tallest beehive Catlin had ever seen. Her uniform was starched brown with a white apron. She padded over to them on orthopedic shoes. "What can I get y'all?"

They ordered eggs, grits, toast, bacon, and coffee. Thankfully, the coffee was served immediately, and they sipped the steaming brew and watched each other in comfortable silence.

She had time to look at his face, the chiseled jaw, the full, sensuous lips. For the first time, she saw a tiny scar on the end of his chin, and she wondered if he'd hurt himself doing one of his special effects. Her gaze moved up his face and she decided that his nose fit perfectly . . . not too big, but not small and wimpy either. And then his eyes. They were wonderful, clear and alive with mischief. They seemed to speak to her as loudly as his voice, and what they were saying made her look away.

"What's wrong?"

How could he read her like that? Was it possible that she was so transparent? "Nothing. I'm just curious about why you wanted to see me. I haven't exactly been the most . . . receptive person in the world."

Luke sipped some coffee and leaned back in the booth. "Last night I did some thinking. You don't want to rush this . . . thing we have going. Okay. I can live with that. I don't want you to run off because I jumped the gun. On the other hand, I'm not going to sit by and waste the days we could be having fun, just because you're scared."

"But. . . ."

"Don't interrupt me now, I'm on a roll. It's pretty clear that we're damned attracted to each other. But I think I can control my raging hormones enough so you don't have to worry every time we go out. Today is the grand experiment. If we can have a good time, enjoy the day and each other without losing control, well, then, I think we can make it through to the end of the picture."

"I see. Do I have any say in this?"

"Seems to me you've had *all* the say so far. As a matter of fact, I think I'm being wonderful, acceding to your every wish."

"Wait a minute." Her back stiffened against the overstuffed Naugahyde booth. "I've gone along with everything *you've* wanted to do. You decide when it's okay to kiss, when it's okay to go out and have fun. Did you ever think I might have wanted to do something last night while you stayed home to 'think'?"

He nodded. "True. Okay, you win. You can take me out tomorrow night. I'll be ready a half-hour after wrap. I like red roses."

She couldn't think of a thing to say to that. Funny how he could leave her speechless. No one in her life had ever made her feel so befuddled. Catlin shook her head and sipped her coffee until breakfast was served and she could busy herself with eating. She watched him covertly during their meal and marveled at the ease with which he not only managed to eat his food, but devour her with his eyes as well. It wasn't uncomfortable, that hungry stare, just . . . intimate.

Luke paid the bill and they hit the road. In a very short time, they were surrounded by wide-open spaces dotted with great old trees hanging heavy with Spanish moss. Even the air smelled of adventure. There was something primeval just under the pungent odor of forest.

The highway ended and they continued along a two-lane road in need of a new coat of tar. She leaned over and turned on the radio. Every station was country, so they listened to country.

"You gonna sit all the way over there?"

She was about ten inches away from him on the large leather front seat.

"I don't bite," he added, smiling.

"I'm not so sure about that."

"Me neither. You better stay there."

How could she resist? She slid over until her hip touched his. Just the feel of his body, not his hands or his lips, was enough to start the butterflies in her stomach. Then, he put his arm around her shoulder. It felt incredibly right, as if it belonged there. Catlin sighed and hunkered down in her seat, allowing her leg to rub against his. The mixture of tension and serenity was something new to her, and she decided to experience it fully. A grand experiment, that's what he'd called the day. Well, she was game.

An old country-western standard came on the radio, and Luke joined in with a beautiful baritone.

He sang almost as well as he played the saxophone. She enjoyed feeling his chest vibrate as he serenaded her.

"Mamas, don't let your babies grow up to be cowboys. . . ."

He was really getting into it now. The animation on his face and the gusto of his voice brought her back to the tour of his truck, how excited he'd been to show her his accomplishments. Everything he tackled was done with exuberance and a spirit of fun.

A typical Capricorn, she tended to be observant and steady . . . a bit aloof. It was wonderful and exciting to be caught up in his enthusiasm. What the heck, she thought, and joined him in the chorus.

They sang and laughed and enjoyed being close as they cruised down the country roads. She nearly jumped out of the truck when he moved his hand onto her knee and discovered how ticklish she was. The look on his face was so full of mischief that she struck a bargain with him: If he promised not to tickle her, she wouldn't strangle him.

The scenery was changing. They passed swamps as large as football fields. Old, rickety shacks dotted the sides of the road. The only hint that people lived there were the large antennae placed high on the rooftops.

"Tell me about yourself, Catlin. You haven't said much about your past." He looked at her with interest.

"It's not terrifically exciting. I was born in Huntington Beach and lived there 'til I went to college."

"Huntington Beach? Were you a surfer girl?"

"You bet. I went every morning before school and every day during summer vacation. Don't I look like a surf bunny?'' She patted her dark hair and fluttered her eyelids at him.

"No." He laughed. "You look like someone who keeps her Barbie doll collection to give as an heirloom.''

"The only Barbie doll I ever owned was sacrificed in a fierce battle between GI Joe and Batman. I wasn't ever into girl stuff. Well, at least not until I reached high school.''

"This is very enlightening. Do go on.''

"Let's see . . . I don't have any brothers or sisters. My folks have been happily married for twenty-eight years. They still live at the beach.''

"Ah, common ground at last. My parents have a great marriage, too.''

"Hard to live up to, isn't it?'' she said softly.

He didn't say anything, but she noticed he wasn't smiling anymore.

"You've been married, haven't you?''

"Oh, yeah. It was a real humdinger of a marriage. Lasted a whole two years.''

"What was she like?''

He was staring straight ahead, and his jaw clenched before he spoke. "Smart, pretty, and when I met her, she was a lot of fun. Then, she got this great job with a Big Six accounting firm, and I guess all those numbers ate away the part of her brain that holds humor. Man, she got into her job in a big way.''

"It must have been difficult, you being away so much.''

"Yeah. It was too difficult. Especially when her ambition came before anything else.''

He looked at her and his wonderfully expressive

eyes showed a pain she'd not seen before. "Can we change the subject?" he asked.

Catlin nodded and looked straight ahead, anxious to let the topic of professional women drop. She couldn't help but compare herself to his ex, though.

Then her attention was caught by something up ahead, in the middle of the blacktop. It was long and low. Luke slowed the truck as they approached the strange object.

"Maybe it's a blanket," he guessed.

"Blankets don't move."

"Maybe it's a blanket covering a dog."

"Good guess. You're probably right."

They inched up the road.

"It's an alligator!" she cried.

Sure enough, a lumbering alligator was making his way from one swamp to another. He moved slowly on squat legs, a few inches at a time. The giant reptile looked about ten feet long and his bottom row of teeth reflected the brilliant sunlight.

"Let's get out and watch him." Luke started to open his door.

"Are you nuts? He could kill us!" She held his arm, but didn't take her eyes from the beast.

"Alligators don't fly. He's not going to leap at us. We can stay a good distance from him, but I don't want to miss this."

"We can see perfectly from the truck. Now, please close the door."

"Do you want me to lock it? Maybe he has a key."

"Don't make fun."

They stared in fascination as the gator swung his immense tail and continued on his way. It was only a few feet in front of the truck when it jerked forward and moved with alarming speed directly at them.

Catlin screamed and Luke jumped so high he hit his head on the top of the cab. She started to laugh at him and, after rubbing the bump on his crown, he laughed, too. The alligator calmly turned back to his walk, having obviously determined that they posed no threat.

"Do you think he's laughing at us?" she asked.

"Yeah. He's probably telling all his swamp buddies about the dweebs in the truck. If I can drive with this concussion, we'll continue down the yellow brick road."

"Poor baby. I'm sure you'll survive."

"Gee, thanks, Ms. Nightingale."

"Drive."

They went on as the afternoon grew tired. It was hard to believe six hours had passed. The sun was touching the tops of the trees and shadows loomed on the great, grassy marshland. Catlin had settled in comfortably next to Luke, her hand resting easily on his leg, her head nestled into the crook of his shoulder. The radio no longer picked up anything but static, so they sat in silence and watched the countryside that was so foreign to them both.

It wasn't only the landscape that was alien to Catlin. The way her heart seemed to beat to the same rhythm as Luke's, and the serenity filling her were a strange, intoxicating blend. Being away from the crew—away from the world—made her feel as if the day had been created as a special treat just for the two of them. As each mile passed, her trepidations fell away like sands in an hourglass. Catlin closed her eyes and inhaled the scent of him, pressing herself even closer to his chest and thigh. Then, she sighed contentedly and wished the day could go on forever.

"Heads up," Luke said.

She opened her eyes to see a gigantic sign on the side of the road: GUMBO! JAMBALAYA! CRAW-FISH! GOOD EATS! FIVE MILES, TURN RIGHT.

"Gumbo, yum," Luke said.

"Great. I'm starving. Boy, I bet they do some business out here. It's so easy to get to."

"Well, I'm glad they're here. My stomach is rumbling so loud, I bet the cook already heard it."

"I sure did." She grinned up at him.

The turn-off road was marked clearly with a flashing yellow arrow. They made their way along a dirt path at a crawl, for the lane was badly pitted. No restaurant was in sight.

"Maybe that sign was put up before the invention of the automobile," Luke said as he inched the truck along. "Hang tight. I think I see something."

Up ahead, to the right, was a large, rambling wooden building with a broad veranda. The area directly in front of the porch had been cleared for a parking lot, and a dilapidated pickup with a flat tire and an unhinged door sat squarely in the center. A cardboard sign, hand-lettered with a jagged scrawl, was fixed to the top of the clunker. It said, simply, "Eat Here."

"Elegant. Just your cup of tea, Luke. I bet they serve wonderful catfish."

He laughed as he parked the truck. A light touch on Catlin's palm stopped her from opening the door. When she turned to look at him, the echo of his laughter made comfortable creases around his eyes and mouth. She felt the urge to trace the lines with her fingertips.

"It'll be great," he said. "We're on an adventure, remember?"

The butterflies were at it again, dancing up a storm inside her. She grasped his hand and squeezed. "You're right. I'm very excited."

His brow lifted.

"About the restaurant." She quickly turned away and waited while he circled the car to open her door. Catlin let Luke help her out of the car, and he held her hand for a moment longer than was necessary. When he let go, she felt as if she'd lost something safe and sweet.

After an invigorating stretch, she looked around and got her bearings. The air was moist and warm and caressed her skin like a silken glove. The stillness of the remote spot was cut by the crunch of dirt and gravel beneath their feet as they walked slowly to the porch. The vegetation surrounding the shack looked weighted by the humid air, and she was aware of the life teeming within the dense growth.

As they approached the steps, the wind picked up and the door of the abandoned truck swung from its precarious perch, emitting a piercing screech of metal on metal. The shadows cast by the trees quivered and made fantastic patterns on the parched soil. What was familiar and quaint a moment ago became eerie as the breeze whistled through the rotted boards, sounding like the mournful cry of a small child.

"Are you sure there's not a sign somewhere saying Bates Motel?" she whispered.

He laughed evilly and rubbed his hands together. "Now I've got you where I want you, my pretty."

"Wrong movie. Although you do make a great Wicked Witch."

They mounted the weather-beaten steps and moved closer to the door. Boards creaked with each footfall, and she found herself moving closer to Luke's tall, muscular body. His arm slid around her shoulder, comfortable and solid, and she released the breath she'd been holding.

"Wait here," he said.

His voice seemed too loud and she brought a finger to her lips to shush him. The arm that had felt so protective was removed and Luke went inside. She waited a moment, then two.

"Luke?" she called softly. She took one tentative step forward, and cautiously grabbed the door knob.

"BOO!" he yelled as he yanked open the door, carrying her forward into his arms.

"You . . . you louse," she said, hitting him with her balled fist. "How mean."

"You weren't really scared, were you?"

Luke caught her arm as she swung at him again. Catlin wanted to wipe the grin off his face. He was holding her tight against him. With each breath, she could feel her chest meet his and her anger turn to heat. She stared up at him, and melted as she saw the desire in his eyes.

She cleared her throat. "Don't you think we should go in?" Catlin fought to conquer her involuntary reactions to the nearness of him. Stepping back, she moved her gaze to her wrist, and the large strong hand that held it. Luke let her go, but she felt the imprint of his fingers marking her flesh as if she'd been branded. When she rubbed her hand, she was shocked that the skin was cool and unblemished.

Luke had stepped back, allowing her to see inside. Before examining the surroundings, she took a surreptitious glance at him and watched as he struggled to regain his composure. He, too, rubbed his hand, and she smiled to herself, knowing the electricity she felt when they touched was a two-way current. With a deep breath, she faced the room.

Tables with red-checked cloths were dotted about, each topped with simple fresh flower centerpieces. Several large wooden fans hung suspended from the beamed ceiling and stirred the sultry air, creating a slight but welcome breeze. A chalkboard was centered on the east wall announcing, in French, the daily specials: *gumbo, jambalaya, etouffé, boudin, saucisse, fromage de tête, gratons les ecrevisses, couche-couche*. A clatter of pots told her someone was in the kitchen.

"Hello," Luke called. "Are you open?"

Moments later, a short, round woman bustled into the dining room from behind a curtain of beads. Her silver hair was tightly knotted behind her head. She wore a red dress, which was roomy and cut at the waist by a stained white apron. Wiping her hands on a dish towel, she hurried toward them on broad bare feet. When she got closer, Catlin saw that her face was as creased as a well-read letter, and that her eyes held laughter behind the folds of wrinkled flesh.

"*Bienvenue, entré, entré,*" said the woman. "Sit. *Vous devez être très fatigué après ce long voyage.*" She indicated a table and gestured for them to sit.

"Do you speak English?" Catlin asked, as Luke held her chair.

The old woman shook her head. "A little. Not

good.'' She rubbed her rounded belly. *"Vous avez faim, non?"*

"Oui," he said, and mimicked her actions, rubbing his stomach with verve. "Jambalaya?"

She nodded, then smiled so broadly they were able to see the gold caps of her teeth.

"Cela ne sera pas long." She pointed to her wrist. This time Luke nodded, then watched her lumber off behind the curtain. He turned back to Catlin. "I told you it would be great."

She marveled once again at his daring spirit. "When you're right, you're right. Is this officially Bayou country?"

"As far as I can tell, we're somewhere near Lafayette. That's the hub of Acadiana. I've read a bit about the history of the Cajuns. They're fascinating people: a mixture of French, African, Spanish, German, English, and Indian."

"What's Acadiana?"

"Cajun is short for Acadian. . . ."

With an unconscious gesture, Luke grasped the chipped vase on the table. While he spoke to her of history and local customs, he drew tiny circles with his thumb on the smooth surface of the glass. Catlin was mesmerized by the motion and imagined her nipple underneath that thumb . . . how his touch would create a fire. . . .

She shuddered, and with great effort forced her eyes up and her attention on the words he spoke.

". . . the original Acadians of Canada came to Louisiana after being expelled by the British."

"Well," she said, trying to make her voice sound natural. "You are a wealth of knowledge. Do you always do this much research, or are you just trying to impress me?''

"I *am* trying to impress you, but not with history." He took his hand away from the vase and folded it over hers. "How am I doing?" His voice softened and washed over her like warm rain.

"Better and better." Catlin met his inquiring stare with false calm. "Today has been wonderful. I can't remember when I've been this happy and relaxed. Thank you."

He kissed her hand with his usual flair, sending tiny shocks through her body, then he yelled for all the world to hear, *"Laissez les bon temps rouler!"* With a wink, he added. "For those who don't speak the *lingua franca*, that means, let the good times roll."

The Cajun woman reappeared, followed by a middle-aged man, both carrying steaming bowls of food. The man resembled the old woman and had the same hurried gait. They reached the table and placed the jambalaya in front of Luke. Reaching into hidden pockets in her voluminous dress, the woman pulled out silverware, napkins, and glasses for her guests.

"Du vin?"

"Yes, please," Luke said.

The man, whom Catlin suspected was the son of the old woman, brought the wine from the back room. It was in a jug and unlabeled.

"I'm Luke, this is Catlin." He spoke a little louder than necessary, as if volume would make the Cajuns understand his words.

"Ah." The woman nodded again. "Margrite," she said, pointing to herself, *"et Henri,"* pointing to her son.

Henri filled their water glasses with rich red wine. Catlin sipped hers and savored the full-bodied taste of the home brew. Then, she tackled the jambalaya. The piquant rice and seafood mixture was spicy hot and delicious. Margrite and Henri beamed their approval, then disappeared behind the curtain.

In short order, nothing was left in either of their bowls. They sat, sated, and slowly finished the hearty wine. She watched as Luke pushed his chair back and stretched his long legs in front of him, crossing his ankles. His movements were languid and his bearing showed contentment. It pleased Catlin to know she was a large part of his happiness. She took another sip of wine and leaned back in her chair, relaxed and satisfied.

The tranquil moment was interrupted when the front door opened and a group of people, all talking in lilting Cajun French, entered the restaurant. One man carried a fiddle without a case, another had an accordion slung over one shoulder, and still another carried an old washboard. The women wore dresses with wide, long skirts; the young girls were more modern in jeans and colorful blouses. The men were all casually dressed in baggy trousers and shirts, and spoke together rapidly as family or old friends do.

Margrite bustled out of the kitchen to greet the new customers. She ushered them to seats near the back wall and pointed to the visiting couple. Luke waved when the entire group unabashedly stared at them.

"Friendly, aren't they?" She moved her chair closer to Luke's.

"They just want to get to know us," Luke said, his eyes gleaming with anticipation.

Some of the younger men began moving tables and chairs, clearing an area for dancing, while others placed seats in a semicircle for the musicians.

Luke got up and helped the men move the furniture while Catlin watched. She couldn't help but compare his lanky good looks to the short, swarthy men surrounding him.

The *patois* was loud and friendly, and delighted her with its singsong tone. Soon, everyone was seated except for a tiny little girl of about two who ran from one table to another, gathering flowers given to her by adoring relatives. Luke came back to the table.

Laughter filled the building, and she heard the sound of an old squeeze-box taking in air. Many feet pounded the floor in quick rhythm as if a hidden metronome had given them the same beat. The pick hit the washboard in double time and the fiddler lifted his bow to join in the music. One of the younger males in the group, a boy of eighteen or twenty, began to sing in a stunning tenor voice.

Luke scooted his chair next to Catlin's, and they tapped their feet and clapped their hands in time to a bouncy Cajun tune. He looked at her almost rapturously, and, at that moment, she felt as if she knew his very soul.

Her heart raced, and she felt as if she would burst with the new awareness inside her. Luke was so in his element in this strange backwoods parish. The people here spoke music and laughter, and he understood both languages perfectly. Happy tears welled up in her eyes, and her throat constricted as she watched his joy.

"I'll be right back," Luke said, as he rose to his

feet. After a wink, he bounded out the door. He returned quickly, carrying his beloved saxophone.

Clapping and cheers welcomed the newest member of the band as Luke placed the sax to his lips. He walked toward the older musicians and joined in, playing as if Cajun music were second nature to him. The washboard player paused briefly to pat him on the back with such force it nearly knocked him into a table. Then, it was on to another tune.

Margrite started to dance, and Henri came up to Catlin and grabbed her hand.

"Viens danser avec moi?"

He pulled her to her feet and twirled her around like a top. Margrite laughed and laughed, all the while dancing on her wide bare feet and swinging her stained apron. Henri was not a particularly fine dancer, but, what he lacked in finesse, he more than made up in energy.

Catlin was exhausted by the time the song ended. She begged off the next dance and sat down to watch the band. She marveled at Margrite's stamina as the old woman danced with the little girl, her large frame moving with surprising grace.

Henri took the opportunity to get glasses of wine for everyone. Catlin stared at her drink and wished for water. She didn't want to be rude to these charming and hospitable people, but the thought of drinking more wine made her uneasy, as she was already a little tipsy.

Before she could decide what to do, Margrite disappeared into the kitchen. When she came back, she brought a clean glass and a pitcher of water to Catlin's table.

"Thank you . . . merci."

"You're welcome, pretty one." Margrite struggled with the English words. "Drink that . . . dance. The night is young."

The evening was flying by in a whirl of song and laughter. Catlin gamboled with every man above the age of five, and some of the women. Margrite and she cut quite a rug on a particularly fast song, and Luke was barely able to play because he laughed so hard watching them.

A ballad was starting, and before two bars had played, Catlin had run to the bandstand and grabbed Luke. He hastily put down his sax and they danced, grinning at each other like wicked school children, happily playing hooky. With only three other couples on the floor, there was plenty of room to move, but Luke didn't seem to need it. He took tiny steps meant to bring them close. He wrapped his arms around her waist and she circled his neck. The grin on Catlin's face faded as she stared at his handsome face. His blue eyes pierced the distance between them, and before she realized what was happening, she was kissing him hungrily.

He responded with an ardor that stopped her from dancing, from moving, from breathing. Her fingers became entwined in his lush dark hair. She pressed her hips into his, and when Luke reacted and grew with desire, she flushed at the proof of his yearning.

Taking her mouth away from his was torture. Looking at him, she felt a great tenderness and a need that was acutely physical. She'd come back to earth with the very real and very frightening awareness of his masculine response. She was responding, too. Her breasts, her thighs, her heart . . . all the places that made her a woman, cried out for relief.

The relief that only he could grant. She stepped away, as if from a heat too intense to bear.

"You shouldn't do that, you know," he said, his voice raspy with desire. "You were the one that wanted to keep it light."

She nodded and looked down, embarrassed to catch his eye. "Sorry," she whispered. "I won't let it happen again."

"Like hell, you won't."

Her head jerked up at the growl that seemed to come from deep within his chest. Luke was breathing rapidly and his lips were pressed tightly together.

"You can't help it, and neither can I. Dammit, why should we?"

Taking her hands quickly away, she turned so her shoulder pressed against his chest, and she laid her head near his heart.

"Because I'm still frightened," she murmured. She looked up at him again. "But not of you . . . I'm scared of . . . of . . . I don't know what. Just don't give up on me, okay?"

He kissed her softly; his lips touched her like a whisper. "Never." He let her go, and walked back to the band.

Catlin felt small and vulnerable on the crowded dance floor. What's wrong with me? she wondered. Why can't I just relax and let this relationship happen? So what if it's just temporary?

The sudden ache in her heart gave her the answer. She'd loved freely, once. The thought of Luke leaving at the end of the movie was already too painful. If she gave all of her love to him, she would never recover.

Luke was with the band now, and he said something to the young singer, who nodded vigorously then spoke quickly to the musicians. Catlin watched curiously as broad grins broke out on the friendly faces and the group turned to Luke for the next move.

Catlin didn't know whether to laugh or cry when the tiny Cajun ensemble started playing the unmistakable notes . . . "I can't get no satisfaction." Evidently, their tête-à-tête had not gone unnoticed, because the whole gang was laughing and looking first at Catlin, then at the crazy saxophone player. She shook her head and joined in.

All too quickly, Luke packed up his sax and let her know they had to leave. To Catlin, it seemed as if she were saying good-bye to old friends. She hugged each member of the wonderful band, and gave a special squeeze to Margrite and Henri. Luke also hugged the mother and son, and they left with a promise to return soon.

They climbed wearily into the truck, and Catlin settled herself in the crook of Luke's shoulder. His arm wrapped around her and became the most secure blanket she'd ever known. They drove away from the ramshackle building and headed toward the state border.

The dark surrounded them as if they were in a cocoon, just the two of them, warm and snug and content to sit in the silence of the night. Before dozing off, she remembered she wasn't supposed to fall in love with this man. Then she smiled and went to sleep.

SIX

Luke whistled softly to himself as he killed the Rebel commander. He punched the board in front of him with a quick and steady rhythm, creating spectacular body hits twenty-feet away. The nasty Rebel fell and died as only movie villains can.

"Cut!"

The director was happy, the actor was happy, the whole crew was happy, but they didn't come close to feeling as good as he did.

Catlin was his! She didn't know it yet, but that was a minor detail. Soon she would discover how right they were for each other, and stop all this dragging-her-feet nonsense. Luke shook his head. It wasn't nonsense to her, and he couldn't forget that. To him, yesterday had been a fantastic coming-attraction. It was so easy to see the two of them exploring Mississippi, working together, playing together. Life was great, and he felt as if he were king of the world.

Luke walked over to the actor he'd just murdered and started to remove the bullets from underneath his heavy coat.

"I'm glad you got such a kick out of killing me. I'll remember that the next time we're alone together." The performer was smiling, but there was a touch of sincerity in his words.

"Don't take it personally, pal. I would have a great time digging ditches today." Luke leaned closer to the wary man and whispered conspiratorially, "I'm in love."

"Congratulations . . . I think *I'll* remove the bullets from my pants. Thanks, anyway."

Luke roared with laughter and walked over to the script supervisor, a crotchety woman who hadn't smiled in twenty years. He swept her in his arms, bent her backwards, and planted a loud, sloppy kiss right on her lips. "I'm in love, Dahlia, and I don't care who knows it."

"Get your hands off me, you cretin," Dahlia hissed. But he caught the tiny grin that lit up her face before he turned to walk back to his truck. He didn't get very far.

"Hey, Luke." It was Michael. He was sipping a steaming cup of coffee next to the catering table. "Let me buy you a cup of java."

"Thanks, buddy." Luke joined the cameraman and poured himself a drink.

"What's the deal with you and Catlin? You done with her yet?"

Luke struggled to keep the smile on his face. "What are you talking about?"

"I was just wondering if the bloom was off the

112 / JO LEIGH

rose. She's one pretty lady, and I was hoping to get my share before the picture wrapped.''

Luke put his cup down and spoke slowly. ''My man, you are truly moving into dangerous territory. As a matter of fact, you're standing over the edge.''

Michael grunted, ''Don't get into a sweat. Old love 'em and leave 'em McKeever couldn't be falling for the boss lady? I know all you want are a few dances in the sheets. Besides, what can *you* do for her career? From what I hear, she's quite the ambitious lady. Hell, it wouldn't surprise me if Peters was already putting it to her.''

Anger flared like a bonfire in Luke's gut. His hands curled into tight fists, which he had trouble keeping at his sides. ''If you so much as think of saying anything like that again, buddy, I'll hit you so hard your whole family will fall down.'' Before he smashed the son-of-a-bitch in the face, he turned and walked to his truck, slowly counting to ten.

It didn't help. He wanted to go back and pummel the bastard. How dare he talk about Catlin as if she were so much merchandise to be passed around the set. Damned camera jockey. He'd known Mike for a long time, and he'd never realized that he was such a jackass.

This business, it was filled with slime like Mike. Everyone just hopping into the sack with the first pretty face to come around. His step slowed. How many times had he been guilty of just that? Too many for his own comfort.

But Catlin. She was different. He had no intention of hurting her. Hadn't he been honest with her from the start? Hadn't she made it clear she wasn't interested in a long-term relationship, either? They were right for each other. For now. And, just because it was temporary, didn't mean it wasn't real. He was in love with her. More in love with her than any woman he'd ever known. Putting a deadline on their time together guaranteed there wouldn't be any bitterness or hurt. They would both leave with a sweet memory. That was the smart way to go, and both of them knew it.

As Luke stood on Bessie's tailgate, he looked across the broad expanse of lawn, passed the cameras and the lights, until he saw the producer's trailer.

Catlin was in there. Working away on revising the script for the umpteenth time. He pictured her crouched over the table, pencil between her even, white teeth. Her hair was probably pulled back, with one or two strands tickling her nose. She would keep brushing it away absently, never taking the time to secure it properly.

Thinking about her rekindled the anger, and he heard Mike's words swimming in his head. What he needed right now was manual labor or a cold shower. Maybe digging ditches wasn't such a bad idea. But he definitely needed something to keep his mind off of that bastard.

"Hello. Anybody home?"

With a start, Luke realized that Stan had been talking to him. He turned to face his young partner. "What's up, amigo?"

"Welcome to planet earth, man. You've been in the stratosphere for about ten minutes. Thought maybe you were havin' flashbacks." He laughed his great, snorting guffaw and Luke laughed with him, although for the life of him, he didn't see what was so funny.

"We gotta get ready for the next fight, dude. I mixed up the blood, but we're out of syrup. You want me to go to the store?"

"Go for it, babe," Luke said. "And don't forget to bring back a receipt."

Stan raised his hand for a high-five. "Excellent. Later, dude. By the way, I fed Harriet yesterday. No, don't thank me. I dig your pig." He leapt down from Bessie and meandered over to Luke's truck, laughing loudly. Each elongated step broadcast that he was too hip to rush and far too cool to be caught up in the excitement of the movie set. Luke shook his head and reminded himself that Stan was the very best he'd ever worked with.

Shrugging his shoulders, he went inside to look for something to occupy his mind and body. First, he'd need to check on his little darlin'. He looked out the back door and found Brandon, or at least half of Brandon. All he could see was a jean-clad behind sticking out of Harriet's house. Harriet was sitting on her rump, patiently waiting for her boy to finish exploring.

"Brandon."

Luke heard a clunk. Then the boy wiggled out of the doghouse.

"Hey, Luke," he said, rubbing his head. "I made her a bed. Wanna see?"

"You bet." Luke walked down the steps and scooped Harriet into his arms, then tickled her in her favorite spot, right under her chin. He allowed Brandon to show him the old, ratty pillow he'd placed inside the little house. The pride he saw in the boy's eyes caused him to pay extra attention to the detailed explanation of how Brandon had found the pillow, washed it, and run all the way to the set without stopping once.

"That's great, son. You've made her real happy." Damn, he thought, why couldn't he look at this kid without his stomach tying itself into knots? He'd heard of biological clocks with women, but never men. Maybe it was just the loneliness he'd felt over the past two years getting the better of him. Or maybe he was still reacting to the fight with Michael. Hell, he was acting like a fool. He put Harriet in Brandon's arms and patted the boy on the head. "I got work to do now. I'll talk to you later."

Luke went back in Bessie. He found the blood mixture on the workbench and checked it for consistency. It was great, as usual. Then he noticed the false walls, and he began the time-consuming and strenuous task of painting the facades so they would match the real plantation house.

Even when his muscles ached and the sweat poured from his skin, he couldn't stop himself from thinking about what Michael had said and wondering just how much of it might be true. Was it possible that Catlin's hesitancy was due to his position? She'd told him once her job was all that mattered. Was that her polite way of saying he didn't fit into her "above-the-line" world?

While Luke painted, Catlin brushed the errant hair from her forehead for the tenth time. Deeply engrossed in the script revisions, she jumped when the trailer door opened and Mr. Peters walked in.

She shifted nervously on the bench seat and tried to read Peters's mood in his stony face. It was no use.

"What are you working on?" This was said with no discernible emotion, so she decided he was delighted to see her. He just had trouble expressing himself.

"Scene twenty-seven. We don't have enough extras to make it work, and I can't spend any more money. We've got to figure out a way to shoot it so it looks as if fifty people are really one hundred and fifty."

Peters threw his duffel bag on the chair and sat next to her. He read the pages quickly, and soon they were engrossed in the tedious process of stealing from Peter to pay Paul. They decided to dress the crew in period costumes and shoot the master from outside looking in. No one watching the movie would ever guess there weren't hundreds of actors.

Hour after hour sped by before Peters finally called a halt to their work. His stomach rumbled so loudly that it interrupted their conversation. She looked at her watch. It was past seven, and she probably would be able to catch the last bus back to the motel. Catlin quickly gathered her belongings and raced outside.

Luke had parked his truck directly in front of the trailer. The door was propped open, and his long legs were stretched out the window, tennis shoes dangling. With his head back on the leather seat and his mouth wide open, his snoring could wake the dead. But he was not alone.

Stan, Sylvia, Dahlia, and several other crew members were standing huddled together near the open door of the truck. Stan waved Catlin over and she walked toward the group, curious to see what they were up to. Dahlia had her Polaroid camera poised, and she waited while Sylvia quietly tied Luke's tennis shoes together. The wardrobe woman froze when Luke stirred, then continued joining the laces after his snoring resumed.

Meanwhile, an electrician had set up a huge light, pointing it so that when it was turned on it would illuminate the truck like the sun. The sound man had his portable playback machine cranked and ready for the signal. A mattress was underneath the door.

Stan held up one finger, then two, and then three. The light came on, flooding the truck with three-thousand watts, and the Sousa march blared so loudly people in the next county could probably hear it. Luke sat up, looked frantically around, and screamed, "Hit the dirt!" And he did, in a beautiful arc, landing face down on the mattress with his feet hopelessly tangled. Dahlia snapped photos during the whole episode. Everyone laughed hysterically and slapped each other on the back, proud as peacocks that the setup had worked so well. Catlin laughed so hard tears streamed down her face.

"One take, guys!" yelled Sylvia. "That was excellent."

"Awesome, dudes. Totally bitchen!" Stan chimed in.

"That'll teach you to keep your hands to yourself," Dahlia muttered as she dropped six developing photos on the prostrate effects man.

"Mmmph," he mumbled into the mattress, before slowly lifting himself into a crouch. He raised his head, looking carefully at each member of the group. "I'll get you. Maybe not tonight, maybe not tomorrow, but I'll get you."

"Yeah," said Stan. "I'm shakin' in my boots."

Luke struggled to his feet, his tennis shoes still

tied together. He caught Catlin's eye. "You. *You* were in on this? Why, I ought to. . . ." he grabbed her around the waist, lost his balance, and they both tumbled onto the mattress. Catlin started laughing again, and couldn't catch her breath. Luke gave in and smiled.

The gang, seeing that the last bus was leaving, grabbed their equipment and hustled to make their ride.

They were alone. Catlin's amusement faded as she became aware of her position underneath Luke. There was a pressure, insistent and unrelenting, between her legs. He'd fallen with his knee pressed against her in a way that made her squirm. She struggled against the intimacy of his hold, but each movement brought him closer. Catlin groaned as she felt her nipples become rigid as they rubbed against his hard chest.

Then his mouth crushed hers, his lips hot and fierce as they fought to own her. His hand was on her breast, kneading her burning flesh while his tongue traced the curve of her chin, then found the hollow of her neck.

She gasped and arched her back, her body taking control of her protesting mind. Finding his chin with her trembling hand, she lifted his face until his lips had once again found hers. And she kissed him with all the passion she'd tried so hard to deny.

The loud bang of the trailer door slamming startled her so much that she bit his lip. Luke moaned and grabbed his wounded mouth. She scurried out from underneath him, patting her hair and desperately trying to straighten her clothes. She was on her feet when Mr. Peters walked past them.

"Good night," she said, stepping off the mattress and trying as hard as she knew how to look completely innocent.

"Uh huh," he grumbled, moving toward his car. He didn't even look up when Luke grabbed her hand and brought her down next to him.

"You bit me!" His blue eyes looked terribly hurt and she moved very close to him.

"Let me kiss it and make it better." She leaned forward and gave him a light peck. Luke's hand moved behind her head, and the friendly kiss threatened to become a continuation of their earlier passion.

"No, hold it." Catlin moved back quickly, afraid that once she got started again, she wouldn't stop. "Not here. Not now."

"When?" His voice was gruff and she could see the struggle in his eyes. "You're making me crazy. I can't keep doing this." He turned his head away and worked at untying his shoes. "I'm sorry, darlin,' but I'm way past the friendship stage."

She rose and stepped off the mattress. "I know." She was glad it was dark, so he couldn't see the flush she felt on her cheeks. "I'm not trying to be a tease, but if . . . no, when we make love, I want it to be just right. You can understand that, can't you?"

He stood and walked her over to the passenger side of the truck. He opened the door, picked her up, and placed her on the seat. "I understand, I sympathize, and I want it to be right, too. But you have to understand something about me." He leaned in so his mouth nearly touched her lips. "I'm in love with you. I'm going to have you. And, honey, I can't wait much longer.''

He pulled his head back and shut the door firmly. She watched him walk slowly around the truck and get in behind the wheel. Without another word, he started the car, and they drove all the way back to the motel in silence.

Catlin knocked on the door to Mr. Peters' suite again. It was nearly midnight, but he'd told her to come over as soon as the new pages were ready. It was just like him to make her stand outside for so long. Catlin leaned against the railing opposite the door.

Exhaustion was taking its toll. The week had turned into a nightmare of logistics. They had worked sixteen hours every day since Tuesday, and tomorrow threatened to go close to twenty. The crew would revolt. Saturday was their night to party, and, if they went passed one A.M., all the local taverns would be closed by the time they wrapped.

For her, the brutal week had been a blessing. It had made it virtually impossible to be alone with Luke. By the time they finished work, they were both so exhausted that all they could think of was sleep. The inevitable confrontation had been delayed, but Catlin's thoughts had never stilled. Whatever she did, wherever she was, Luke was on her mind.

She'd pushed herself harder and harder, taking on tasks that rightly belonged to the production coordinator or the unit manager, just so she would fall in bed and sleep. And not have time to think about how his lips had tasted, how her insides had turned to fire when he touched her.

The door opened, and she straightened, focusing on the papers in her hand. She looked up when she heard a feminine gasp. Standing in the doorway, dressed in a man's robe, was Vicki, the assistant director. Her hair was tousled and her face was flushed. "Uh, hi, Vicki. I've got some pages for Mr. Peters." This was very embarrassing. She didn't know whether to run, or act as if she expected to see the young woman open her boss's door.

"Oh, um . . . I'll get him." She shut the door in Catlin's face. After a few minutes, Mr. Peters opened the door and asked her in. Vicki was nowhere to be seen.

"You've got the work?" Peters was as brusque as usual. He didn't seem to mind that she'd found a woman half his age in his room.

"Here. It's complete. As soon as you sign it, I can get it over to. . . ." She realized that the pages would naturally go to Vicki.

"I'll see that she gets them." There was no hint of irony in his voice. He scanned the changes and initialed each page. They both stood, she more awkwardly than he. "They're fine. Good night." He left her standing in the middle of the sitting room, while he entered the bedroom.

"Good night," she said to no one. She let herself out and closed the door with a loud bang.

Back in her own room, she thought about her boss as she got ready for bed. Just that afternoon she'd heard him talking to his wife and his young son. Through the grapevine, she'd learned his third marriage was a good one and that he adored his two-year-old boy. Vicki must surely know he was a married man.

Was this what all movie marriages were like? What if she and Luke were to get married? Inevitably, they'd get different shows, which would mean a separation of weeks or months. Would he be strong enough to avoid temptation? Would she?

Catlin climbed into bed with the questions swimming in her head. Even if she were foolish enough to let herself fall hopelessly in love with Luke, what made her think he'd want a wife who was a professional? Hadn't he said that's what had broken up his marriage? There was no way she was going to give up her career and, obviously, careers and a love life couldn't possibly mix.

Catlin only hoped her job would be enough.

Saturday morning came too quickly, and Catlin forced herself out of bed and into the shower after the third buzz of her alarm. As it had been for the past several weeks, her first thought was of Luke. He, too, would be in the shower now. The image of his lean, muscular body wet with slippery soap was so disquieting that it woke her completely, and she hurriedly finished bathing and dressing. She made herself list her duties for the day. It was the only way she could stop herself from thinking about him. She ran downstairs and caught the crew bus just in time.

Sylvia waved and she sat down next to the wardrobe woman.

"How are you, cookie? Ready for another glorious day of battle?" Sylvia asked.

"As ready as I'll ever be." Catlin leaned back against the cold plastic of the van seat.

"I've got some juicy tidbits for you." Sylvia turned on the seat so she could whisper her gossip.

"Alan, the director of photography, not Alan the prop guy, moved in with Terry. You know, the makeup girl who came on late? Anyway, he moved in with her, but what he didn't tell her was that he was moving out on Denise."

"Who's Denise?"

"Actress? The one with the big . . . ?"

"Oh, yeah."

"And, talking about actors, it's supposed to be hush-hush, but our stunning leading man and leading lady are taking their roles *very* seriously. Rehearsing day and night."

"Really?" Catlin felt wicked listening to all the gossip, but it was hard to stop Sylvia once she got on a roll. And, if Catlin were really honest with herself, she had to admit she found the information fascinating.

"And, last but not least, our favorite stunt coordinator, Cody, has decided one of the wranglers is his new true love."

Catlin raised her eyebrows.

"A gorgeous female wrangler. I can't remember her name. Stephanie, maybe. Anyway. That's the early edition of the Natchez news." She looked at Catlin through narrowed eyes. "Unless you have something to add?"

Catlin shook her head. It was bad enough that she enjoyed listening to all the gossip, but she wouldn't participate. Sylvia obviously didn't know about Peters and Vicki, and for some reason, she was glad of that.

All this talk about the personal lives of the crew made her wonder what was being said about her relationship with Luke. It must be common knowledge, but so far only Sylvia had talked to her about it face to face. Oh, and Peters knew, but Catlin doubted he cared at all.

She could tell Sylvia wanted to talk about Luke, but Catlin wasn't going to bite. Luke and Sylvia were old friends, and she knew that he confided in the wardrobe mistress. Let him tell her what was going on. That would be safer for everyone.

The bus stopped near the production trailer and she said good-bye to her friend. The first thing she looked for was Luke's truck. There it was, parked in front of Bessie. And there was Luke. He was wearing his faded jeans, as usual, topped with a sweatshirt that had the arms cut off. She watched him lift the heavy wall from his truck and hand it down to Stan. Even from this distance, she could see the muscles in his arms bulge and she imagined the sweat trickling down his back.

Help! She turned away and practically ran to the door of the trailer. She had to stop thinking like this. *Work. Keep busy.* She didn't even bother to grab a cup of coffee before she opened her script and read with every ounce of concentration she could muster.

Fifteen pages later, Mr. Peters walked in. He was all business, as usual. They poured over the board and watched the videotapes of the previous week's shooting. The filming was going well. The next two weeks would all be night shooting, beginning at five p.m. and wrapping at five in the morning. The only concern was the weather. A major storm was supposed to be coming their way, but, with luck, it would begin and end on Sunday. If it lasted, they had "cover" sets ready to go, which could be filmed indoors.

At noon, the phone rang and she picked it up. Mrs. Peters asked for her husband, and Catlin held the phone out to him. She tried to stop the flush that covered her cheeks, but Peters was too quick. He caught her embarrassment, and his thin lips narrowed to a flat line before he grabbed the phone. She busied herself with the work before her and tried to ignore the conversation he was having with his wife, but the room was too small. Every lie he told made her wince.

How could someone do something so underhanded to a person he supposedly cared for? But she knew that answer. Hadn't it happened just like that to her? She felt terribly sorry for Mrs. Peters. If she had any brains, she would kick the bastard out. Just like Catlin'd kicked out Craig.

Yeah, right, she scolded herself. She'd fallen for his lies like a naive babe in the woods. She'd never had the chance to kick him out because she hadn't discovered his treacherous deceit until the very end. And that, more than anything, had burned her right to the core.

Catlin thought about what she was doing with Luke. Was she being just as foolish as Mrs. Peters, as Vicki, as the gorgeous wrangler who had hooked up with the stunt man? This was a location romance, no different from her relationship with Craig. If she didn't keep remembering that, she was in for more pain than she could imagine.

Who was she trying to kid? It was already too late. She could no longer deny that she was in love. And not like any love she'd ever experienced before. She needed Luke, like she needed air to breathe, food to eat. How would she ever survive the end of this movie? As sure as Catlin knew she would make love to Luke, she also knew that a large part of her heart would die forever once they said good-bye.

Peters hung up the phone and turned to her. "About Vicki. We both know this is just a location thing. My wife knows that when I'm on the road, these things happen. It's no big deal."

She turned from him to hide her reaction. Warring thoughts rumbled through her brain. He was lucky to find a wife willing to stand behind him. But how could he do this to her? Catlin fought down the words that threatened to pour out of her. Think of your career, she told herself. Keep it all inside. She wouldn't let this petty man jeopardize all she'd worked for.

His voice grew more brittle as he continued. "Grow up, honey. You want a life on the road, this is what you get. You think no one's noticed your little fling with Luke? It's not like he's going to marry you, right? And you're bright enough to know that if he did want to get married, you would be losing a hell of a lot in the bargain. You're management. And we all have our perks. So, do me a favor, and don't play Miss Self-Righteous." Then he grabbed the board and walked outside.

So, it was no big deal . . . a bonus for making it in the big time. Love on the road was nothing, as phony as the play-acting they worked on all day. The facades, the practiced lines; those were the reality. Why had she let herself believe, even for a minute, that she and Luke had a future? She knew better than that and she had still let herself forget the lessons that Craig, and Hollywood, had so painstakingly taught her.

Slowly placing her script inside her portfolio, Catlin's chest tightened as she thought of the words Luke had spoken that night in the truck. Maybe he did love her, but she must get used to the fact that it was only for awhile. That would have to be enough.

The storm hit that night. Lightning flashed so near she felt the hair on her arms stand up. The rain came down in sheets, as thick as a wall. It hurt her skin as she rushed, with the other members of the company, to cover all the equipment and bring all the props indoors. The tired and drenched crew were dismissed at two A.M. She didn't even bother to look for Luke. She got on the crew bus, and struggled to stay awake until she could reach her room. Her soaked clothes lay in a puddle next to her bed as she crawled between the sheets, naked, shivering and alone.

The phone woke her at noon. Luke's voice made her clench the cord between shaking fingers.

"Hi, sweet face. Can you come out to play?" He sounded so damn cheerful . . . and so very wonderful.

"No, thanks. Today is a perfect day to stay in bed."

"Great. I'll be right over."

She laughed. "No, you won't. I'm curling up with a good book, and I suggest you do the same. Neither of us can afford to be sick, and I know you were as wet as I was last night."

"Okay, mom. I'll drink my tea and put on my slippers. But don't you think it would be loads more fun cuddling together?"

A sharp image of Peters' face came to her. His

harsh words reverberated in her mind. "Not today. I need to be by myself. Okay?"

The pause was painfully long before he spoke.

"Sure. I'll catch you later."

She heard the click on the other end of the line, and she hung up the phone. Her breath caught in her throat and she turned and buried her head in the pillow, tears stinging her eyes.

It was a long time until she could stop crying. Oh, God, she thought as she tried to catch her breath. Why does life have to be so complicated? Was it possible for two people to fall in love and stay that way without hurting each other deeply? Was it all Hollywood make-believe? They made their living creating illusions. Was she making a mistake in believing that what had developed between them was real?

She fell into a troubled sleep as the wind howled outside her window. When she woke, she looked at the clock, but it wasn't working. Neither was the table lamp. She scrambled out of bed, grabbed her robe and opened the front door. It was pitch black outdoors. Why weren't the lights on . . . anywhere? The rain had stopped and the air was hot. The humidity must be close to ninety percent, she thought. Making her way over to the phone, she dialed the front desk. "Could you tell me the time, please?"

"Around eight p.m., ma'am. What room is this? We'll bring up candles. The whole city is blacked out. Don't know when we'll have lights again."

"I'm in room 207."

"Someone will be by in a few minutes."

She felt her way over to the dresser. Blindly, she put on jeans, a shirt, and sandals. Groping along the walls, she found the bathroom and washed her face. It took a minute to find her towel, and she stumbled over the commode. Where were those candles?

A knock on the door came to the rescue. "Just a minute," she yelled. The urge to rush was sharply curtailed when she banged her shin on the side of the bed.

"Damn! Hold on, I'm coming." She hopped to the door, massaging her injured leg. "I'm so glad you're here."

"Great. I'm glad to be here."

She looked up and saw Luke holding a hurricane lantern next to his smiling face. He carried a blanket and a bottle of wine in the other hand. Next to his foot was his trusty saxophone.

"Follow me. I know the way to paradise." He kicked the sax lightly. "Mind giving me a hand?"

She picked up the case. "Wait. Where are we going? I need my purse."

"No, you don't. Just be quiet and come on. I've never led you astray before, have I?"

"Well, no, but there's always a first time."

He walked down the corridor, the lantern illuminating the walkway with an eerie yellow light. They reached the stairs, and he led the way up. They climbed four flights until they reached a heavy door. He pushed it open, and bid her enter with a dip of his head.

They were on the roof, but it felt as if they were at sea, for nothing was around them except brilliant stars and massive dark clouds. There must have been a full moon, because she could see the outlines of each billowing cloud as if they had been etched with a laser beam. Never had the heavens appeared so close.

Catlin reached out with her hand, as if to catch the nearest star and keep it next to her, always.

Luke walked to the center of the tarred roof. He laid the thick blanket over the wet surface, and she sat down. From his back pockets he withdrew two champagne glasses and placed them in front of her. He uncorked the sparkling wine with a loud pop and poured them each a drink, then lifted his glass for a toast.

"Tonight, my love, I'm going to tell you how I feel. Everything that's in my heart. And you're going to listen."

SEVEN

Catlin watched Luke take his saxophone out of the case and put the strap around his neck. His languid movements were silhouetted against the stars and she could feel her chest tighten as he turned to face her. The sultry night air stroked her skin like smooth black velvet and she rubbed her hands over her arms as a shiver borne from excitement, not cold, skittered over her body. She studied him and tried to memorize how he stood with one hip a bit higher than the other . . . how small his waist was compared to the inverted pyramid of his shoulders . . . how his hands caressed the keys of the saxophone with patience and power.

She couldn't find the right position for listening to his music. She squirmed and fidgeted, finally kneeling with her hands braced on her knees.

Luke stepped just out of her reach, and in that moment Catlin knew the power he held over her. He could hurt her more deeply than anyone in the world,

131

but it didn't matter. He could also satisfy the desire that was making her tremble . . . He could fill the void that had made her life empty.

He could love her.

"This is for you, Catlin. Your song." He brought the sax to his lips.

As the first note rang out, piercing the silence of the night like an arrow, her heart raced and her stomach tightened. The melody captured all the quirky moods of the man who wrote it. Each time she thought she knew where the song was heading, it changed direction and made her smile with surprise and delight. He hypnotized her like a snake charmer with his music, and her body swayed to the sensuous rhythm. His chest rose, expanding the thin material of his shirt. The fabric boldly clung to the muscles Catlin ached to touch. His mouth held the instrument firmly, and she licked her lips as she imagined herself replacing the saxophone in his arms.

Luke took a step closer to her, and the impact of his masculinity made her dizzy. Her body tensed with wanting him, her breasts tightened and throbbed underneath her shirt, and she grew moist between her legs.

"Oh, my God. . . ." she whispered.

He stopped playing, and she fell into the stillness as if she were a feather drifting in the wind. When she came back to earth, he was there to catch her. Breathlessly, she watched Luke move toward her, and her arms reached for him, her body aching.

"You're so beautiful, my sweet Cat," he said, his voice raspy and low. "Tonight, I'm gonna listen to you purr."

The next moment she was standing in his arms,

her lips crushed beneath his hot, wet mouth, his tongue hard and probing. The knot that had been in her chest exploded into millions of sparkling lights as she met his ardor with her own. Catlin quivered as he ran his hands over her back and cupped her buttocks, pressing her against his swollen manhood so she felt his fire through their clothes. Then, his hands moved roughly around her waist and up until he captured her breasts. He squeezed and caressed the sensitive nipples until she wanted to scream. All the while, he kissed her, his tongue teasing her until she heard a low moan and realized it was her own voice pleading.

The full moon had come shining through the clouds, and she could see his eyes burning with undisguised passion. His mouth was moist, inviting her to take her pleasure.

"My dreams were never this wonderful." His voice was as steamy as the humid night air.

Catlin reached between them to undo the bottom of her shirt, but she lost patience with the buttons and lifted the blouse over her head, dropping it where they stood. Luke's hands closed over the tender skin of her breasts and he moved his thumbs to draw tiny circles on her erect nipples. She gasped and her chest rose to meet his hands. Then her eyes closed and her head lolled back. Catlin was drowning in feelings and his touch was her lifeline. Luke used both hands to pull off her pants, bending his head forward and kissing her softly on each breast, sending shivers of electricity coursing through her. Then his mouth continued down her belly until he reached the soft triangle of hair where his hot breath penetrated the inner folds of her flesh.

It was agony waiting for him to pull off his own clothes, so she helped him—tearing at the belt buckle, ripping his shirt in her eagerness to have him naked against her.

Finally, they both were undressed, their hot bodies melding under the canopy of stars. She was once again gathered in his arms, and his mouth was on her lips, her cheeks, her neck. His hands roamed freely, touching her thigh, her breast, her knee.

She touched him now, her fingers teaching her all she longed to know: how his skin was like satin and his muscles were like steel. He took her hand and guided it down until she felt the heat of his loins, then he let go, and she explored his rigid shaft.

Luke moaned and brought her down on the blanket beneath him. He reached over to his discarded pants and found the pocket. He pulled out a silver packet and quickly ripped it open, then slid the condom over his throbbing flesh.

"I need you," he whispered urgently. "I'm sorry . . . I can't wait."

He braced himself above her, and with one smooth stroke he entered her and she took him in, expanding to encompass all of him, finding that she was made to hold him.

"Cat . . . oh, God . . . my love. Tell me that you want me."

"Yes . . . yes. I do want you."

He thrust and the sweat of their bodies joined together; their juices mingled in the most intimate of dances.

It was all he could do to control the pace, not to go crazy and fill her and fill her until he exploded. Luke breathed deeply, the heady scent of Catlin sending him spinning, and once again he had to taste her mouth, her skin. She was so soft that he couldn't believe she wasn't something from his dreams; no woman could be this incredible and want him, need him. But she did. "Tell me again. Tell me that you want me."

"I want you, Luke. I . . . love you."

He kissed her then and tasted salty tears. When he looked at her, he saw the love in her face, and his chest knotted with a tension he didn't want to feel.

The sex had changed. He was no longer an animal in heat, he was her lover and all that existed for him now was her pleasure.

Catlin grasped the back of his head and brought his mouth down on hers. She was naked, truly naked before him, and she wallowed in the vulnerability and the power it gave her. She couldn't stop the tears spilling down her cheeks. Whatever happened, she did love him. Nothing could change that.

The heat inside her built, coming close to that crescendo she longed for. Was her love for him strong enough to bring down the walls that distrust had built, allowing her to have the release she so fervently wanted?

His thrusts grew more urgent as he neared his climax. She smiled when he deliberately slowed his pace to wait for her. Gripping her muscles, she raised her hips and increased the pressure . . . this would be her gift to him.

Luke's hands grasped hers and pulled them over her head, then his back arched. He was slowly building up and up, his whole body shaking as he drove into her. And then he let go, his body gave a final tremor and, spent, he lay his head on her bosom.

"I'm sorry." His voice was barely a whisper.

"For what? That was glorious. And, I love you."

He lifted his head and looked into her eyes, searching. "You didn't. . . ."

"It's fine, really. Next time. You have to understand something about me, Luke. I would rather be really with you, like we just were, than find a million G-spots. It's the closeness that I want . . . and the trust."

"I don't see why you can't have both. If I'm doing my job right."

She moved her hand slowly across his cheek, then patted his silky hair. "It's not about your job, Luke. It's about trust. Next time will be for me."

He clasped her hand in his then moved up her body until his mouth was just above hers. "I'll hold you to that."

He kissed her. In the silence of the evening he heard a very soft, deep purr low in her chest, and he smiled. But somewhere in the back of his head he kept hearing her words . . . *It's about trust.*

They lay entwined. Catlin burrowed her head in the crook of Luke's shoulder, listening to the steady rhythm of his heartbeat. With one finger, she traced lazy patterns across his rising and falling chest, bewitched by the motion and the feel of his skin beneath her hand. Her leg was flung over his thigh and he massaged her knee with his free hand, sending pulses of warmth radiating from her leg all the way up her body.

"Oh, sweet mystery of life, at last I've found you," Luke warbled in an off-key falsetto. She laughed and clapped her hand over his mouth.

"So much for afterglow."

"This *is* my afterglow. You'd better get used to it."

He lifted her gently with him as he sat up, their naked bodies shimmering under the soft light of the moon.

"Isn't this just the most perfect night? I'm gonna have to figure out how to black out the city so we can do this again."

"I'm sure the electric company will be pleased."

Just then, the lights came back on and the magic cloak of the night was gone. Catlin leaped up to grab for her clothes, while Luke slowly stood up and stretched lazily, not caring in the least that he was buck-naked.

She threw his pants at him, which he caught one-handed. "Put on your pants, you show off."

From below, the sound of hundreds of voices cheering rose up and filled the night air. People had come out of their homes and shops to applaud the return of the lights.

Luke bowed, sweeping his arm across his waist, letting his pants fall to the blanket. Then he turned to face the other side of the roof and bowed again. "Ah, my adoring public. It was nothing, just a bit of the old McKeever magic."

She laughed again as she zipped up her jeans. "If you don't put on some clothes, that McKeever magic will have to help you disappear from jail."

"Don't be silly." He picked up his clothes and dressed while keeping his eyes on her. "No one can see us, we're on top of the world."

She smiled. "We sure are."

Moving close to him, she rubbed her hands over

his chest, enjoying the feel of the now-familiar muscles beneath her palms. He leaned down and kissed her, his lips rekindling the fire that lay just below the surface. Her hands continued their leisurely exploration, moving up to his shoulders, then around his neck.

His tongue swept across her teeth lightly, teasing her until she opened her mouth and bid him enter. He thrust his hands into her hair and crushed her to him. She responded to his urgency, meeting his with her own tongue and pressing her hips into the hardening flesh of his body.

"Your room." He stared at her with smokey eyes as his desire echoed hers. "Let's run."

They parted and quickly gathered up the blanket, glasses, lantern, and sax. Then they dashed to the door, raced down the four flights of stairs, and entered her room, laughing and gasping for breath.

Catlin collapsed on the bed and when she turned to look for him, she saw that he was leaning against the closed door, watching her and smiling.

"What?"

"You're gorgeous. And sexy. And I want you."

She patted the bed. "Come sit down."

Luke shook his head. "If I take one step closer, I won't sit and I certainly won't sleep. It's got to be at least two A.M. We won't be able to function at work."

Groaning, she turned over and buried her head in her hands. "Go. Get out . . . hurry."

She heard the door open and close. Then open again. He was suddenly next to her, his hands were lifting her and she was in his arms. He kissed her lips, her nose, her cheeks—a hundred tiny kisses like the patter of rain on her face.

"Sleep is highly overrated, don't you think?"

"Mmm. Let's at least pretend to sleep."

"Okay." He jumped on the bed with all the grace of a lummox and smiled winningly at her. "I give great cuddle."

Catlin lay down next to him and maneuvered herself until she was comfortably aligned with the angles and planes of his body. While her head rested on his shoulder, she ran her hand underneath his T-shirt and rubbed the flat expanse of his stomach. She enjoyed the feel of the warm, soft flesh, and the awareness that she could, with perfect abandon, touch any part of his body she desired.

"Don't you think we'd be cooler without these clothes?" Luke whispered.

"Only for about two seconds. We're supposed to rest, remember? If you're a good boy, I'll give you cookies later." She looked up at him. His hair was disheveled and a dark stubble covered his chin. She'd never seen a more handsome man. "We can talk, though."

" 'Bout what?"

"Tell me about yourself." She closed her eyes and shifted her hip, finally finding the perfect position.

"Okay. I was stolen from my parents as an infant, and raised by gypsies who taught me all of their secret sex rituals. . . ."

She yanked his chest hair.

"Ouch."

"Want to try again?"

"Spoilsport. Don't blame me if you fall asleep." Luke ran his fingers lightly down her arm. "I was born in Colorado and lived there until I was sixteen. Then I moved to L.A. to work with my uncle. He taught me special effects. You know, he worked on *Gone with the Wind*. Anyway, I traveled with him as an apprentice for six years. He got me into the union. Then I went on my own, got some jobs, and the rest is so incredibly boring even I can't stand to listen to it.''

''Where did Susan fit in?'' Surprised that the question had come out so abruptly, she quickly glanced at his face. He was staring at the ceiling and she couldn't read any emotions.

''We met in L.A. when I was working on a TV series, got married after a few months, and then I started traveling.''

He paused for so long that she looked up at him again. He was still implacable, but his jaw was more rigid. The movement of her head seemed to jog him back to the present.

''Things didn't go so well after that. She couldn't travel with me because of her job. But she wanted a house and nice cars, and the only way I could earn that kind of money was by working locations. I don't know. It sure wasn't what I thought marriage was supposed to be.''

''And what's that?''

''You know, I work hard all day and come home to a hot dinner reservation and an attentive ear. We struggle and save so we can take vacations in the Poconos. Eventually, we have a couple of tax-deductible kids and a dog named Sparky.''

''Just like June and Ward Cleaver?''

''Right. Only she didn't see it that way. Believe it or not, she ended up working more hours than I did. We hardly ever saw each other, and even our phone calls were infrequent. Our life styles were not copacetic, if you get my drift.''

''Well, I can't see what's so wrong with someone having career ambitions. Surely, you must have known what she wanted before you got married.''

''Yeah. Sure. I knew she wanted to work, but I didn't think her job would be *all* she wanted.''

''So, you want a woman who'll stay home and raise kids?'' Catlin's heart was beating too fast. She wasn't sure she wanted to hear his answer.

''I didn't say that. Marriage isn't in my plans, and . . . this is not my favorite topic. Let's talk about something else.''

Catlin heard his words, and a small part of her died. But, she thought, she'd known the truth all along, and she couldn't blame him for stating it. No, she'd made her decision, and even though there was no possibility of a future with Luke, she was his for now. She'd deal with the parting when it was time. Tonight, she would love him, and take whatever he could offer. ''What should we talk about, then?'' she asked, glad her voice was sure and strong.

''How about if it feels good when I do this.''

His hand went between her legs, and she wiggled until he captured her in a kiss that stopped her struggling.

The morning was unbelievably beautiful. Catlin stood outside the wardrobe tent and stared at the marshmallow clouds covering the sky. Her skin tingled in the crisp air of early morning and she felt like singing. She turned, entered the huge tent, and smiled at Sylvia.

"Isn't it a stunning day?"

"Yeah, stunning. I have to dress twenty-five women in bustles and antique dresses and finish in one hour. It's a real peach of a day." The small woman scurried across the dirt floor, grabbed a maroon velvet dress from the rack, then eyed Catlin. "This one should do. Come on and get dressed."

"Me?"

"Yes, you. Everyone wears a costume today. You're the one who gave that order."

Catlin remembered that she had, in fact, issued that instruction a week ago. They needed the bar scene to look packed with extras, but the budget didn't allow for any more than the fifty they'd already hired. She took the gown from Sylvia.

"Do I need any special undergarments?"

"Nope. You'll be a dance-hall girl, they didn't go in for bustles. Lucky you. Now, get changed, and don't bother me anymore." Sylvia was off again to help a matronly woman lace up a stiff whalebone corset.

Catlin admired the plush velvet of the low-cut dress and went behind the partition to change. She took off her slacks and shirt and slipped on the period costume over her bikini panties and lace bra. She felt the pull of the Civil War era, made real by the musky smell, and the weight of the dress and the hem reaching her toes.

Her bra, however, was showing above the dropped decolletage. It was awfully low-cut! She peeked around the screen, looking for Sylvia. Perhaps there was something a little more conservative for her to wear.

In the main room it was chaos. Women in all

stages of undress were frantically trying to find the right shoes or a matching hat. And Sylvia was in the middle of the storm, working on three women at once.

Ducking back into her private enclave, Catlin shrugged her shoulders and removed the offending undergarment. The amount of bosom showing above the rich folds of material was disconcerting. Could she walk around like this and not be arrested?

She went into the main room in search of a mirror. Impatiently, she waited while many other costumed women checked their dresses, then stepped forward to see how much of her was going to be on film.

The ensemble was magnificent. The rich velvet made her skin look like cream and the tight bodice gave her a tiny waist. As for the neckline . . . she was decent, but barely. She pulled the garment up, which helped a little. It was far more daring than she would ever choose herself. But it did make her feel very sexy. Luke would sure like this dress.

"Sylvia," she called. "What about shoes?"

Catlin had finally finished in makeup and hair, and she felt like Belle Watling walking through the old-time saloon. The appreciative stares she was getting from the men on the set made her walk with a bit more swing in the hips than her usual gait. The huge bar was filled with cameras, lights, props, and extras. The set decorators had gone all-out in their selection of antiques to capture the mood of the 1860s, and they were panicked that in this crowd an expensive piece would be broken or stolen. The director was hoarse from yelling at the crew and the assistant director was using the bullhorn to try and get some quiet.

Where was Luke? He should be setting up for the fire scene that would burn the building tomorrow night, but she didn't see him anywhere.

She located the false wall behind the bar. She knew it was false because she'd been in on the design work, but to the naked eye, it looked perfectly real. Only when she glanced behind the counter did she see that the wall stopped just below waist level. And there she found myriad pipes, wires, and jets that would control the fire.

She peeked underneath the facade and saw a Union soldier working on a pipe fitting. She studied the long legs and the small derriere and smiled. "Luke?"

He turned and grinned at her. "Hi. Like my uniform?"

"You bet. Come on out here and I'll show you mine."

He put down the pipe and walked to her, but instead of joining her on the noisy set, he grabbed her wrist and pulled her under the divider next to him. They were hidden from the crew in the very tight space, and his arms went around her waist, sweeping her close enough to kiss.

The hot, demanding pressure of his mouth made her shaky. The stroking of his tongue against hers made her squirm with a need so intense it was almost unendurable. Her hands went up to his neck and her body pressed against his. All it had taken was one kiss, and she was wet with wanting.

Catlin broke away and tried to catch her breath, but her heart was pounding and her pulse raced. "We can't do this here. I have work to do, and so do you.

Besides, there are a hundred people on the other side of this wall.''

"Screw 'em.''

He kissed her again, and she heard him groan deep in his throat. She worked her hands down so they were on his chest. She could feel the steady thump of his heart through the material of the costume. Gathering her willpower, she pushed him until they were separated. "Luke, not now.''

He dropped his hands to his side. "Okay. I'll go back to work.'' A devilish smile curved his lips. "How about a nooner?''

She slugged him in the shoulder. "Stop that. You didn't even notice my dress.''

"Notice it? I wanted to rip it right off your body.''

"Oh, you silver-tongued devil. You certainly know how to sweep a girl off her feet.''

"That's the point.''

"I'll see you later.'' She quickly ducked under the wall and composed herself before seeking out her boss. It took a moment until she was sure her cheeks were no longer red, and the desire for Luke had left her eyes.

It was difficult to see past the throng of bodies, so she stood on tiptoe and swept her gaze over the crowd, but stopped when she caught a glimpse of overalls ducking behind an arc lamp. Brandon. Maneuvering between extras and crew members, she quietly snuck up behind the crouching little boy. He must have sensed her approach because he made his move, but he wasn't quick enough. She hung on to him tightly while he squirmed.

"What did I tell you about sneaking around? This is a bar, Brandon, and there's no way you can be in this scene. We have too much work today. I can't be chasing you all day."

He appeared to be properly chastened, but she knew he would sneak in again at the first opportunity.

"I'm going to call your mother. She'll take you home."

"You can't." He smiled, and she grew even more suspicious.

"Why not?"

"Because she's here. I have to stay. Ain't got no one to watch me."

"I see. Well, you go find your mamma and stay next to her. Don't be running around, or I'll have to ask you both to leave. Do you understand?"

He nodded his head sagely. "Yes ma'am. I promise not to run around."

"Okay. Go on."

The youngster flew across the room, bumping into tables and people with equal abandon. All she could do was sigh, and look for her boss.

There was Peters. He stuck out like a sore thumb in his safari jacket and tan slacks. Of course, she thought to herself, *he* wouldn't put on a costume. She crossed the room, weaving between the equipment and the full dresses of the ladies, until she reached him.

"Mr. Peters. I'm going to stay on the set today, unless there's something else you need me to do."

He turned to her with his customary scowl. "The mayor and the city council are all here. Make sure they have a good time. I'm going to the trailer to watch dailies. Let me know if something goes wrong."

She nodded. "I've never met any of those people. Could you introduce me before you leave?"

Peters didn't answer her, he just walked toward a group of older men and women, all costumed, and motioned her to follow. She had to run to catch up with him.

"Mr. Mayor, this is Catlin Clark. She's the associate producer and she'll take care of you today. She can answer any questions or get you what you need."

He left her standing with the group of dignitaries, and she introduced herself all around. "I think I know a good vantage point for you. Follow me."

She led them back to the bar and positioned them carefully, so they would be seen on camera. Then she went behind the bar where she could whisper to them and have it look natural on screen.

Luke would also be closer, but she didn't mention that to her guests.

Catlin leaned forward and placed her elbows on the bar. She quickly hid her cleavage with a bottle of whiskey. Then she pointed out the different actors and crew members as they walked by. The dignitaries were thrilled to be on a real movie set and asked her question after question about the filming process. Finally, the camera moved so her little group was center stage. During this take, they were to mime speaking so the room appeared busy, but the actors could be heard.

As she feigned a conversation with the mayor, she felt something brush her dress. Her skirt was being lifted, slowly but surely. No one could be behind her—except Luke. He was raising her dress!

She felt her cheeks start to burn. She couldn't turn

around or slap at his hands because the camera was right on her. If she blew the shot, it would look terrible, especially in front of the whole city government!

Oh, God! His hands slipped under her panties. Catlin knew no one could see behind the bar, but she still felt as if he was seducing her on camera. She tried desperately to keep her composure, but as his hands grew more intimate on her naked flesh, she began to stutter and gasp.

Suddenly, the mayor lost his grip on the glass he was holding and it fell behind the bar, right next to Catlin's foot. Automatically, he began to hoist himself over the rail to retrieve his prop. Catlin blanched and found she couldn't catch her breath. He would see everything! She turned to block his path, but before she could reach him, a disembodied hand rose up beside her and placed the glass quietly on the counter. Without blinking, the mayor took his tumbler and continued acting up a storm.

This is what a heart attack feels like, she thought. She was as red as a lobster and madder than hell. *I'll kill him.*

"Cut!"

The word rang loudly in the hall, and before she could turn, her skirt was dropped. She whirled around, but he was gone. She was aflame with embarrassment and didn't offer an explanation to her guests. She just squeaked out an "Excuse me" and darted away.

Where was he? He deserved to be murdered. But how? The skunk was hiding, but he'd have to come out, sooner or later. She walked outside, letting the morning air cool her down. Revenge. That's what she wanted. She glanced around, watching the beautifully dressed extras parade between the wardrobe tent and the set. Then she smiled.

Luke stepped out of the honey-wagon after Catlin had passed by. He couldn't stop chuckling at the dirty trick he'd pulled on her. Well, whenever this movie ran on TV, she'd have something special to remember during this scene. And so would he.

The feel of her skin underneath the thick velvet had made him so hot for her, it was all he could do not to get carried away. He'd needed the protection of the wall as much as she did, for his lust had become quite obvious.

Wow, was she ever mad. He was in for it. But that could be fun. The image of her attacking him with all her might, and where that could lead, was rather enticing. He laughed out loud. What a rotten thing to do! He loved it.

The bar was still a madhouse and he searched the crowd until he saw the maroon velvet dress. There she was, alone in the corner, her back to him. He made his way across the packed room until he was just behind her. The corner she was in afforded them enough privacy so she could hit him if she wanted to. He owed her that.

What the heck, he thought. One more for good measure. Quietly, he reached around her and grabbed the enticing flesh of her bosom.

She twirled around, dislodging his hands—but it wasn't Cat! A woman he didn't know was looking at him, ready to kill. She pulled back her arm, and with stunning precision, clipped him on the chin with enough power to send him reeling.

Then he heard the laughter. Massaging his aching jaw, he turned and saw Catlin, laughing so hard she was crying—and she was wearing a green dress!

Through her laughter she said, "Luke, I'd like you to meet Tina, she's the stunt woman we hired for the fire scene."

Tina looked nothing like Catlin from the front. Their hair was the same color, and done up in the same twist, and they were the same height, but that was it. This woman was attractive in an earthy sort of way, but no match for Catlin.

"How do you do? You've got a great arm."

"Thanks, captain," said Tina. "You've got pretty good hands yourself." Then she turned to Catlin. "All even, Cat?"

"Yes, thanks. I owe you one."

Luke moved closer to her. "You mean that? We're even?"

She studied him for a moment before answering. "No. I don't think so."

"Maybe you should slug me yourself."

"It's tempting. But I'm thinking about something much worse."

"Oh, really? What would that be?"

She started walking toward the door. "What time is it?"

"Nearly twelve, why?" He followed her, but cautiously.

"Because that's lunch."

Just then the assistant director yelled lunch over the megaphone. Catlin turned and ran from the bar, and Luke chased her, wondering what he was in for. She was running like the wind, lifting her heavy skirt in both hands, and he saw that she was barefoot.

Soon they were past the lunch truck, heading for the slave shacks built for the movie. Of course, they were empty now, and wouldn't be used again for another two weeks. She must know that. He grinned. She also knew the shacks had beds in them. He ran faster.

EIGHT

Catlin reached the slave shack just before Luke. She leaned against the side of the rickety building and took great swallows of air. Looking down, she saw her bare feet covered with mud. Her laugh caught in her throat as she struggled to fill her burning lungs with oxygen.

Luke came up behind her and reached out to grab her shoulder, but his arm dropped like a lead weight. He bent over, held his side and gasped for air. "I . . . didn't know . . . they had a marathon . . . in Natchez."

The fire in her throat was just calming down as she looked at him and shook her head. She could have responded, but it wasn't worth it. Luke had straightened up and was staring at her. His brow lifted and a smile worked the corners of his mouth.

Catlin looked over his shoulder, pointed her finger back toward the set and said, "Look."

He turned to follow her pointing finger. She shot

passed him, ran quickly inside the wooden building, and slammed the door shut. Two seconds later he was banging on the door. She pressed her body against the flimsy barrier, knowing she wasn't strong enough to keep him out for long. A quick glance around the small room showed her nothing but a cot and a table . . . nothing very inspiring. She hadn't thought about what she would do once she got into the shack. Her gaze went back to the bed.

Luke pounded, causing her to jump as the wood shook under his fist. "Open this door, Miss Catlin." He was speaking in the most ridiculous Southern accent she'd ever heard. "My troops are posted outside, and I can break down this door. I have a weapon."

She turned and peeked between the wooden slats. The only thing she could see was a sliver of his shoulder. "I know all about your weapon."

He laughed. "Then you'll let me in."

She tiptoed quietly until she was perched on the edge of the low table. Luke burst in with such force that he ran all the way across the room and hit the back wall. Her laughter was loud in the tiny room and was joined by his low, hearty chuckle.

She stared into his sparkling eyes and saw his need for her. It grew quiet. Her insides tightened, her pulse quickened and heat ran through her, centering deep in her abdomen. She looked first at his face, then down to his chest and admired the old-fashioned uniform. There was something about a man in uniform, no matter what era. The rich blue cloth strained against his broad shoulders and hugged his narrow waist. She looked lower still and saw more evidence of his desire.

Catlin tore her gaze away and looked up. Their eyes met as Luke approached. His rapid breathing sounded raw and expectant. The potent scent of him washed over her. All that existed were the two of them and the overwhelming power of their desire.

His lips crushed hers and their tongues met in a passionate dance. The force of his body shifted the table until it braced against the wall.

He frantically lifted the front of her thick velvet dress. Meeting the obstacle of her panties, he ripped the thin material from her body. She struggled with the buttons of his pants, tearing two in her haste to have him free.

The kiss didn't stop, and the taste of him made her wild. He pushed her legs apart with his and in one powerful move he thrust himself inside her. She gasped as he drove his hardness deep into her moist opening. His hands went to her breasts and he caressed the exposed flesh, then moved his fingers inside the garment until he reached her hardened nipples. The rough texture of his fingers against the sensitive tips made her shiver.

She ran her hands over his shoulders, feeling the muscles tense with each lunge. Luke let go of her breasts and moved his hands under her dress until he held her buttocks. Then he lifted her until she was no longer sitting on the table, but was supported entirely by his hands.

Grasping the thick material of his uniform, she held onto him and raised her legs until they were wrapped around his back. He was steel as he slowly moved her up and down on his rigid shaft. The sensation was so intense she wanted to scream.

Catlin began to quiver, and she tensed her muscles

around him so that each motion was unbearably tight. Each nerve in her body was sensitized and the smallest movement drove her crazy. He quickened his pace, moving faster and faster, her breath a staccato accompaniment, until finally, she convulsed in a release so profound she cried out as if in pain. She heard him moan and felt the shudder of his body as he, too, let go.

All she could hear was his ragged breath in her ear. Her body continued to tremble as she slowly lowered her legs and stood with her arms still wrapped tightly around his neck. Before he withdrew, he found her mouth and kissed her sweetly, the light contact of his lips offered like a prayer. They parted but still she clung to him, needing the feel of his arms and the touch of his body.

"I. . . ."

Catlin closed her eyes, and felt his lips kiss each eyelid tenderly. "I love you, too."

"I want to be with you . . ."

Her heart leapt at his words.

". . . for the rest of the show. I want to move into your room."

Tears sprang to her eyes and her chest constricted as the words he spoke registered in her dazed mind. For the rest of the show. Not forever. It shouldn't have hurt. She'd certainly been prepared to hear the truth. But it did. It hurt like the devil. There was no way she was going to let her foolish romantic fantasies ruin everything. She'd made the decision to be with Luke, knowing full well that it was temporary. "Let's not make that decision now. Let's just enjoy this moment."

He wiped a tear from her cheek and kissed her

softly on the lips. "Much as I want to stay here, we'd better go back."

She nodded, and just looking at his face, his happiness, made her disappointment ease. She straightened her clothes, concentrating only on the pleasure she felt when she was with him. It was enough.

"My underwear!" she cried as she picked up her torn panties. "What am I supposed to wear?"

Luke snatched the garment from her hand and shoved it in his coat pocket. "I'll think about you being naked under that dress for the rest of the night."

She stood for a moment, embarrassed and excited all at the same time. "It better not get windy."

He roared with laughter and grabbed her around the waist. They left the shack and hurried back to work.

The day stretched on, filled with scene after scene in the crowded bar. Catlin was able to sneak a few private moments with Luke when they happened to meet in a hidden corner or behind a wall. Stolen kisses and a lack of underwear made the whole world feel spicy, and she wondered if the crew bustling around her could sense the air of eroticism that surrounded her.

Catlin didn't know what to do with her crazy emotions. She loved being with Luke. He made her feel more alive than she'd ever dreamed possible, but she knew herself well enough to know she wasn't the kind that "did" affairs. She was a one-man woman, and so far, she'd broken all of her cardinal rules. When she was with him, nothing else seemed to matter. It was when she was alone that the future made her weak with fear. Would she be able to get over him? Or would she spend the rest of her life comparing all men to Luke, and finding them all wanting?

She shifted on her stool to catch a glimpse of him across the long hall. He was engrossed in an animated conversation with Stan. His hand kept wandering back to his pocket—the pocket that held her torn silk underwear. Embarrassment made her flush, and she crossed her legs tightly. Just thinking about making love to him made her breasts throb.

Thankfully, she didn't have to do any work with Peters, for she was in no condition to be businesslike and proper. Her thoughts were as far from proper as possible.

"Hi." It was Luke. The smile on his face was devilish.

"What have you been cooking up this time?"

"Dinner." He held up a bottle of champagne and his grin became very self-satisfied. "Join me?"

"You clever man. How ever did you arrange a picnic? I know you haven't left the set."

"Yeah, but Stan did. It was all set up before you arrived this morning. Come on, we can sneak out of here now and no one will be the wiser."

"What if I'm needed?"

"You won't be." He took her hand and hurried her through the throng of extras. They made it out the door and onto the wide expanse of lawn without being noticed.

Ducking between trucks and past the production trailers, Luke led her through a small gate onto a rolling hill dappled with low-hanging trees. The grass was so green it looked as if they were in the middle of a golf course.

"Nice, huh?" Luke asked.

"Gorgeous. What is this place?"

"A private garden. It belongs to one of the land barons out here. Stan made friends with the guy's son. We have permission to dine here any time we want."

"Good for Stan."

"There it is." Luke pointed to a particularly large tree and he picked up the pace. They jogged over a slight rise and came upon an idyllic setting: a large blanket was spread out under the branches, a picnic basket was holding down one corner, and an ice chest held down another. There was only one thing wrong with the picture: Brandon had discovered the treasure and had made himself at home. And he'd brought Harriet with him! They caught the boy with a chicken leg in one hand and a piece of pie in the other. The pig was busy working on an ear of corn.

"You little . . . I'm gonna tan your hide, boy," Luke yelled.

Brandon sat frozen like a deer caught in headlights. He didn't even finish his bite.

"Mmm howwy."

"Take the food out of your mouth," said Catlin.

He gulped. "I'm sorry."

"Sorry won't cut it this time," added Luke. "Who said you could take Harriet out of her pen? And how did you find this place? It's private property."

"We followed Stan." Tears were gathering in his big green eyes. The poor thing looked so pathetic that Catlin couldn't stay mad, and when she glanced at Luke, the look on his face told her that he couldn't either.

"Do we have enough?" she whispered to Luke.

"I suppose so," he said with a great sigh. "Okay, you little rug rat. You can stay. But next time, ask."

"Okay, Luke. Thanks." He took a huge bite of pie, and most of the cherry filling hit his shirt, instead of his mouth.

Catlin sat down next to the tree. Luke opened a linen napkin with a flourish and laid it across her lap. Harriet raced to her master's arms, anxious to be petted. He gave her a quick tickle, then found the half-eaten corn cob. When Harriet was settled in, Luke handed Catlin a glass and popped the cork on the champagne.

Brandon's eyes grew wide as he watched Luke serve her the dinner he'd prepared. "I never seen no guy do the servin' before."

"Guys do lots of things, Brandon. You keep a sharp eye out today, and maybe you'll learn something." Luke handed the boy a plate. "One of the first things is how to use a napkin. No young lady likes a messy man." He sat near the boy and carefully wiped the food off his cheeks.

His ease with Brandon surprised Catlin. It was as if he'd been around children his whole life, but she knew he didn't have kids of his own. Perhaps his family had been large. There was something incredibly tender about the way the big man wiped the hands of the little boy. He'd be good with a son, she thought. He'd be good with our son.

Catlin looked away. That was a thought out of the blue. One thing she had been sure of was that children were in her *distant* future, if at all. After she was a producer, after she'd made her mark . . . that was where children fit in. Not with the special effects

man, either. Especially not with a man who wanted
no part of marriage and a family. But, my, their
children would be splendid. "Luke, why don't you
eat. We don't have much time."

He dug into the food, and soon the three of them
were talking and laughing, and she couldn't help but
pretend they were a family, complete with pet pig.
Even if it was just make believe, it felt very, very
nice.

By the time they got back to the set, most of the
extras had been released, so it was pretty quiet
around the trucks and tents. Luke went inside to return Brandon to his mother, and to take Harriet back
to her pen, while Catlin walked over to the craft
service table and poured herself a cup of coffee.
Nothing like lukewarm coffee in a Styrofoam cup to
warm a girl's innards. After examining the rest of
the spread laid out for the crew, she was happy to
stick to the drink. Stale donuts, broken cookies, and
half-empty bags of potato chips made her appreciate
the wonderful picnic even more.

She looked around. Just behind the wardrobe tent
stretched a long expanse of lawn. It looked cool and
inviting, and she couldn't resist. Her feet were still
bare, and when she reached the grass, she wiggled
her toes in the scratchy plush turf and released a
large sigh. She sat down and thought about the last
two days. A delicious shiver shot through her and
settled where she sat.

She remembered their late-night talk. His humor
had made her smile, but something about their conversation wasn't quite right. The more she pondered

his explanation for the breakup of his marriage, the more concerned she grew.

He'd obviously not been able to deal with a wife who was a professional. It was as if his ideas about marriage had been formed in the 1950s. But that didn't match the terrifically supportive man she knew. Their conversations had always been as much about her job as his. And he'd made a point of acknowledging her for a good day's work or a money-saving idea. No, something was out of whack. Perhaps it was Susan. Maybe there was more to their story than Luke had shared.

That was a neat rationalization, she thought. It was that kind of thinking that had gotten her in so much trouble with Craig. She turned her attention back to the set, and discovered that a new lighting setup was being rigged. That meant at least a fifteen-minute break.

Why did she have to spoil one of the most perfect days of her life with all this thinking? Couldn't she, just once, relax and enjoy herself and not over-analyze the situation until it was squeezed dry?

Luke had never done anything that wasn't kind and thoughtful, and God knows, always truthful. She had walked into this relationship with both eyes open. It was absolutely useless to keep thinking about a future with the man. It only made her crazy. Besides, he'd never fit in with her plans. After all, she was going to be a producer, wasn't she? That meant constant travel and crazy schedules. He'd never agree to put his career on the back burner, just to be with her.

The thought stopped her in her tracks. In the space of two days, she'd gone from trepidation to marriage plans . . . and thoughts of children! Was all this just because they had slept together?

No. It was because she loved him.

The truth of that statement doused her like a bucket of cold water. She was in love. With a man whom she barely knew, whom she would never see again after this movie was finished. Great. Now what? The next scene was probably ready to start so she hurried back toward the bar, but stopped just outside the wardrobe tent. Get back to work. That was the smart thing to do. Let the affair cool down, let her set her priorities again. It would be tough, but she could do it . . . had to do it. Her life was finally planned, with each phase of her career plotted neatly, and love was not included. Love messed everything up.

She looked at the door to the set and caught a glimpse of Luke, so dashing in his captain's uniform. Then she went to the wardrobe tent and quietly asked Sylvia for a pair of panties.

Catlin tried to concentrate on her paperwork. It was difficult to think about anything except the war going on inside her. Her heart was telling her to go to Luke, be with him, love him, while her head was just as insistently prodding her to proceed with caution and not be a fool. So far this morning it was heart, one; head, nothing.

Last night had been relatively easy. By the time they wrapped, both she and Luke had been dead on their feet. His simple good-night kiss had warmed her, and she'd fallen asleep quickly. This morning was another matter.

During the ride to the set she'd been quiet. She

watched him, the little scar on his chin, how he bit his lower lip when waiting for the light to turn green, how the tendons in his hand bulged when he turned the wheel of the truck. And she realized how much there was to learn about the man she loved. Did he read science fiction, or adventure stories, or mysteries? What was his favorite food, color, song, ice cream? Did he love her?

All other questions fell away like leaves on an autumn day. *Did he love her?* She couldn't escape or stop the persistent query from repeating itself over and over in her head. Even now, four hours after they had arrived at work, the same four words haunted her.

She knew for certain that she was crazy about the guy, and that her judgment had been pretty awful in the past. The only other love in her life had been a world-class jerk. Her ruminations were interrupted by Peters, who stomped into the trailer. His total lack of social grace had ceased bothering her weeks ago.

"Get out the board. A new weather front is coming in and we'll have to use cover sets for at least four days. That means no fire, no rescue scene, no exteriors at all this week. We'll shoot the bedroom crap and then the school. What does that do to my actors?"

Catlin took a second to adjust to the barrage of information. The task in front of her was overwhelming; every person working on the film would be affected. The paperwork alone would keep her there most of the night. Well, there was only one thing to do. Take one step at a time and break down the problem into manageable pieces. Together, they began the painstaking work of reorganization.

Late that night, after the rest of the crew had been released, Catlin was still hard at it. Her coffee had grown cold, and the thought of trying to revitalize the already stale brew made her stomach churn. Peters had left at seven, presumably to work back at the motel, but she guessed what he was working on was a hot meal and a sultry blonde. Suddenly, the trailer was too cramped, the air was too stuffy, and she couldn't bear one more minute alone.

She gathered up her papers, stuffed them into her briefcase, and left the tiny room for the first time since early morning. The air outside was heavy with moisture and the night was very dark. She felt as if she'd been forgotten, and it hurt to see that Luke hadn't waited for her. Of course, they hadn't spoken at all during the day, and he had no way of knowing she was still here, but it hurt just the same.

If he really loved her, he would have figured out where she was and come to rescue her. Her white knight didn't come galloping by, so she walked over to the transportation tent and called the teamster captain from his portable phone. She found him in the dining room of the motel, and he told her to sit tight, that a driver would be there in ten minutes.

She settled into one of the folding chairs to wait. Then the quiet moved in. No traffic noise, no yelling crew members, no machinery grinding. The only sound she heard was the sharp hum of the crickets as they sent out their love calls. After a great sigh, she allowed her mind to wander.

With a start she realized that for most of the day Peters had followed her lead. Without a conscious effort on her part, she'd taken on the role of supervisor. A sense of great satisfaction swept through her. Work was the one place where she didn't have doubts, where she knew she could count on herself. No raging insecurities about her job kept her up nights—not like the other parts of her life. She was fine with friends, and her family relations were on an even keel—and then there was romance. All of her confidence and her ability to make good decisions went flying out the window when it came to love.

Just then, she saw headlights bouncing across the dirt road heading in her direction. She gathered up her belongings and walked out to meet the car. As it approached, she saw that it was a truck . . . Luke's truck. Ah, Lochinvar.

He stopped right in front of her, leaned over and opened the door.

"Going my way, lady?"

She climbed in next to him and kissed him lightly. "Home, James."

"As madam wishes." He winked then turned his attention to getting them back to the motel. "You were sure busy today. I didn't even see you at lunch."

"We had to change the schedule. You know about the weather, right?"

"Yep. Should be an easy week for me. I only have two fires to build, and they're both in fireplaces." He turned to her briefly. "What about you? Gonna have any time to relax?"

She shook her head. "No rest for the wicked."

He gave her a lazy smile. "Damn straight. And I intend to keep you as wicked as possible."

"Not tonight, big guy. I've got miles to go before

I sleep. All I'm going to do is curl up with a warm shooting schedule.''

"Want company? I do a mean back rub."

She immediately became aware of the tension in her shoulders, and imagined his large, warm hands massaging her aches away. "That sounds heavenly. But no hanky-panky. I've got to get some sleep."

He held up three fingers. "Scout's honor. Well, maybe some hanky, but definitely no panky."

She grinned. "Hey, how did you know I needed a ride?"

"I just happened to be in the dining room when you called. Actually, I put out an APB when you didn't come in on the crew bus. Peters told me you were still at work. By the way, I was talking to him about an idea I had for the fire scene. I want to burn the slave shacks in back of the big house, too. Then we can show the slaves being forced to save their master's home, while all their belongings go up in flames. Great idea, huh?"

"Sounds good. I have to check on the budget, though. We may not have enough money to do that."

"I'm not worried. I've got friends in high places."

She smiled, but not enthusiastically. "I'll talk it over with Peters."

They reached the motel and Luke carried her brief-case to her room. As soon as the door was closed, he dropped the bag and folded her in his arms.

"God, I missed you."

His hand moved to the small of her back where his warm palm massaged her tight muscles. He leaned back just enough so he could seek out her eyes. Then he moved his other hand slowly up her arm until he reached her neck. Pausing briefly to brush a loose strand of hair clear, Luke continued the lingering journey and his fingers caressed her cheek, her temple, the bridge of her nose. All the while, his eyes never wavered. They were soft and intense all at the same time; hiding a question just behind the promise. Catlin turned, closing her eyes, until he cupped her chin with a gentle pressure.

"What's wrong?" His voice was barely a whisper. He guided her face until she once again was caught in his gaze.

What could she tell him? That she was scared? That her heart wasn't ready to be broken again? That love hurt too much? Her skin burned where he'd touched her. She heard her own breath become raspy and erratic. Her hands trembled as she clutched his shirt, her grip so tight that her fingernails were digging into the flesh of her palms. She released her grasp and brought her arms to her sides. "I'm tired and I have work to do." With one step she moved away from him; she felt the small distance turn into a gaping chasm.

"What did I do?" Luke watched her walk away, confusion and pain making his gut ache. He felt as if he'd been punched in the stomach. This was the same Catlin who had loved him under the stars, the very woman who had made him go crazy in the slave shack, but now she was a stranger to him.

He racked his brain, searching for a reason, but he found nothing. "God dammit, don't do this, Cat. Talk to me. Tell me what's wrong."

She walked slowly over to the bag he'd dropped on the floor. Without looking at him, she picked it up, carried it to her bed, and pulled out her script. The bound paper shook in her hand.

In one stride he crossed over to her, grabbed the script from her hand and threw it across the room. He took hold of her shoulders and forced her to face him. His grip eased when he saw the tears that streamed down her face.

"Please, baby. Don't cry." He used his thumb to catch a tear as it slid down her cheek. "If I've done something, it wasn't on purpose. If you tell me what it is, I'll apologize."

"You didn't do anything. I just can't see you anymore."

Another punch, this one right to his heart. "Why?"

She took the bottom of her shirt, raised it to her eyes, and wiped away the moisture and the black smudges. When she released the once-pristine material, it was crumpled, wet, and stained.

"My services are no longer required? I'm not needed anymore?"

"No, God, no." She shook her head and reached her hand toward him. "It has nothing to do with you. It's me. I . . . I can't love you and walk away."

NINE

Luke sat down next to her and took her hand in his. "Why are you worrying about that now? We've got weeks to be together."

She laughed. "Weeks."

"You know it wouldn't work for us to plan further than that. But, jeez, Cat. It's so great *today*. Why borrow trouble?"

She sat quietly for a moment, and he watched her take a few deep breaths. He wished he could help her—ease her fears. When she finally spoke, he had to lean forward to hear her.

"I fell in love, once. On my first location shoot. He was older than me, established. A producer. Craig was everything I thought I wanted—smart and handsome and a powerhouse at work. We went together for four months. We roomed together, worked together. I really thought I was in love, and that he loved me back. He wasn't like you. He never said we'll be over when the picture's over. He let me believe that it would go on forever." Her voice had become brittle. "On the contrary. To hear him talk, marriage was just around the corner. He talked about us as if we were a team, you know?" She finally looked at him. "I gave him everything . . . all of me. As long as I knew Craig loved me, I could face anything. Except for his good-bye."

Her words caught him off guard. The tightening in his stomach spread to his limbs, and he lurched off the bed and began to pace, trying to ease the strain. She'd been in love with another man and a big wheel at that. All he could think of were the women he'd said good-bye to. He'd told them all the truth—that he wasn't the type to stick around—but that never seemed to matter when it came time to leave.

"I made a complete fool of myself," she continued. "I made plans for the future. I even went so far as to plan our wedding. I was high for weeks knowing that soon I would be Mrs. Craig Anderson.

"The movie ended, and it was time to go back to L.A. I should have guessed something was wrong when he took an early flight. I thought that was about work . . . that he had to be in editing right away, but it had nothing to do with the film. It was his way of saying so long, Toots, thanks for the ride.

"When I finally got hold of him, he acted as if I was some kind of moron for not realizing it was all a location thing. He'd never had any intention of staying with me."

Tears fell freely from her eyes. She didn't move to wipe them away, or disguise the pain in her face, and seeing her that way made him aware of his own pain—and anger.

"I had to stay with the company until my job was

over. Every day I saw him, and every day he acted as if we'd never been anything more than casual friends. Oh, but he did give me a great recommendation. I suppose that should have been enough.''

What he felt wasn't sympathy. He could feel the rage growing inside him . . . that bastard had destroyed so much. But was he any better?

"I'm sorry, baby. But I'm not Craig. I'd never lie to you.'' The words came out more harshly than he'd intended. He sat down next to her and put his hand on her shoulder, but she twisted out of his reach and stood, hugging herself.

"That's not the point. Don't you get it? I'm no good at this. I can't just pretend nothing has happened between us! Well, okay. I can face the world as it really is. But not yet. Not with you. Please, if you have any feelings for me at all, let me go. I don't think I can make it when. . . .''

She couldn't speak anymore. The thought of him leaving her at the end of the movie filled her with such agony that she couldn't say the words.

Luke stayed on the bed. It was hard to look at him because all of her pain was echoed in his face. She wanted to go to him, comfort him, but her feet froze on the carpet.

"So, it would be better if we'd never met. Never had the kind of effect we've had on each other. You can give it all up and not care?''

"Who said I didn't care?''

He stood up. "You're acting as if I've done something horrible. That caring about you and loving you was wrong. Well, I'm sorry, but I can't agree with you. I'd rather have a moment of really being with you than a lifetime of playing it safe.''

Playing it safe. The words hit her square in the gut. Was that what this was all about? Was fear making her ruin the best thing that had ever happened to her? She closed her eyes because she couldn't seem to think straight when she was looking at him.

She peered into her future . . . to an endless stream of motel rooms and lonely nights, to never knowing love at all because there would always be the chance that it would end in pain.

Luke was right. He wasn't Craig, and he hadn't lied to her. Maybe all she would ever get of true love would be this time with him, and here she was throwing it away. There was plenty of time to go through the hell of being without him—all the rest of her life. Did she have to start now? Didn't she even deserve a few more weeks of happiness?

She felt him next to her, and she opened her eyes. The look he gave her was filled with the kind of ache she knew all too well.

"Cat, I can't tell you I'm gonna change. I probably won't. I'm not good for the long run. And you and I, we're heading in opposite directions . . ." He stopped talking to take a breath. "But you've got all I can give. For now."

She reached out to him and traced his lips with her fingertip. "Shhh. I know. God help me, I know." Then she was in his arms. And there was healing in his touch.

Their pliant kiss merged his love with hers. She knew, despite any pain to come, that for now she was his. His hand ran down her back until he reached her knees, then he lifted her and carried her to the bed. He laid her down gently and then lay down himself, moving so he was right next to her.

"Just hold me," she whispered.

He wrapped his arms around her and held her close, rocking her gently. "It's okay, baby. We'll be fine," he whispered.

Sheltered next to his body, Catlin buried her head in the crook of his neck and allowed his gentle words to soothe her. Her eyes were closed and she concentrated on calming down. Her heart finally stopped pounding and fell into a gentle rhythm that mimicked Luke's.

Three more weeks. That's all the time she had left with him, she thought. Three weeks to love him and be loved. That had to be enough. She'd remember everything. His music, the wonderful day in the backwoods with alligators and Cajun dancing. The magic of the rooftop. The memories would have to be enough.

She made a silent vow. *For the rest of my time with Luke, I'll make every second count.*

She moved to look up at him. His face was filled with an infinite tenderness that made her feel right about her decision.

A door seemed to open in her soul. It was as if a haze had been lifted and she could see Luke clearly for the first time. He was here with her now—not Craig—and this beautiful man was offering her his heart. It may not be the "happy-ever-after" she'd dreamed about, but it was honest and true. Maybe she was a fool, but for the first time in years she felt herself opening up to love.

"You all right?"

His voice seemed to come from far away. She nodded. "Let's really enjoy the rest of the film, okay? I won't mention Craig again, or anything negative. We'll just have fun.''

He frowned. ''That's not what I want. If something's bothering you, tell me. If you're sad or depressed, I'll share that with you. I'd like to be able to tell you everything, too. Just because it's not forever, doesn't mean it isn't the real thing.''

She smiled and kissed him on the lips. ''Yes, sir. There's something you can share with me right now.''

He ground his hips tighter against hers. ''I was hoping you'd ask.''

She pushed her hands against his shoulders and created a little distance between them. ''What I want to share is some dinner.''

''Foolish choice, but okay. I can handle that,'' he said with a wink.

He rolled off the bed, leaving her feeling adrift, but his smile buoyed her.

''Anything special you want?''

She shook her head. ''Whatever.''

''One whatever, coming right up.'' He walked to the door, but turned back to her before leaving. ''You sure everything's okay?''

''Everything's wonderful. I love you.'' Catlin said the words quickly, but as her chest warmed, she was assured that she'd spoken the truth.

''Be right back, love.''

The door closed behind him and the room fell into silence. Catlin sat up and stared at the script laying crumpled next to the dresser. She had work to do. Hours of it. But all she wanted was to be with Luke.

Stop it, she thought. She got off the bed and straightened her clothes. Work is forever, Luke is

. . . stop that, too. Just get going. She picked up her briefcase and the script and spread her worksheets across the bedspread. Within minutes, she was hard at it.

The knock on the door startled her. She let Luke in and grabbed one of the trays he was carrying. They went to the small round table in the corner of the room and sat down. He unrolled their silverware from the paper napkins and poured two sodas.

He was sure about things . . . sure about her. Maybe for a while she could lean on his broad shoulders. It would be nice to depend on someone else, even for a short time.

"I thought you were hungry."

She came out of her reverie with a start. "I am." She looked at her meal for the first time. Catfish! She had to laugh.

"What?" He looked at her, puzzled.

"Nothing. This looks wonderful." She moved her parsley to cover the staring eye of the ugly fish.

After dinner she went straight back to work. The new schedule finally came together and she called each department head with the changes. By the time she was done, it was after midnight. Luke had been sitting quietly absorbed with a book during the hours it had taken her to finish the job, but his presence made her feel safe. It was only after the last piece of paper had been put away that he moved from his chair.

The first thing he did was run a bath for her, using her shampoo to make bubbles. She didn't mention the huge jar of expensive bubble bath perched on the counter.

He helped her out of her clothes. As each garment hit the floor, she felt as though she were shedding her worries about work, one by one. She crawled into the steaming tub, closed her eyes and tried to relax her aching muscles, but she quickly realized Luke had other plans. He joined her in the too-small bath, causing the water to slosh all over the floor.

He sat facing her, his naked chest dotted with the white froth of the bubbles. "I do a mean front rub, too."

His eyes remained on her face while he took the bar of soap from the holder and brought it to her neck. With long, slow strokes he washed her; the cool soap made her skin feel like the softest petal on a perfect rose.

"Mmmm, this feels wonderful," she said. "Whatever you do, don't stop."

"No need to worry, darlin.' Just relax and let yourself be putty in my hands."

He continued his leisurely tour of her chest, then moved below the water.

Catlin closed her eyes and let her other senses take over. She heard the gentle lapping of the water against the side of the tub, smelled the rich lavender scent of the soap meld with the clean, sharp odor of the bubbles. But mostly she felt every inch of her body contract, then relax, as Luke gently, soothingly plied his magic.

If only she could capture this moment and replay it again and again, like a favorite movie or a beloved song. Perhaps her memory would be good enough, but how could a reminiscence take the place of his very human touch?

She opened her eyes. As soon as she looked at

him, her courage was bolstered. She took the bar of soap from his hand and returned the gift he'd just given her. After a few moments spent lathering his chest, enjoying the feel of his muscles and chest hair beneath her sensitized fingers, she dipped beneath the water.

It was time to end the bath.

The rains came late that night. Catlin was awakened by a clap of thunder that rocked the room and made the windows rattle. A flash of lightning illuminated the dark room and she caught a momentary glimpse of Luke's sleeping figure.

He was on his side with his arms clutching his pillow tightly to his stomach. His naked torso seemed to shimmer, with a golden cast that remained etched in her eyes even after the lightning had dissipated. She moved closer to him and reached over to touch his shoulder. He was warm and reassuring in the darkness.

Catlin listened to the torrent that fell outside, the wind whipping the trees into a frenzy and the rain slapping against the concrete. A shudder coursed through her, and she carefully removed the pillow from between Luke's hands and folded herself in his embrace, spoon fashion. He didn't wake up, just adjusted his legs so they were comfortably entwined with hers.

As she relaxed in his arms she thought about what had happened after they had come to bed. Her body still carried the traces of his love: her chin was scratched from his five o'clock shadow, her muscles ached from reaching, straining, and her heart was still filled with desire and passion. Even when he lay next to her, asleep, she longed to be closer again. He made her feel complete.

To be without him would leave her unfinished.

"I've got a proposition for you."

Catlin stopped writing and waited for Mr. Peters to continue. He'd been silent since morning, and she'd been tense all day. The rain hadn't helped. Each drop was magnified as it hit the metal roof of the trailer and the fierce downpour hadn't let up. The room felt stuffy, and the atmosphere in the cramped quarters had put her on edge. What could he possibly want now?

"I'm doing a new TV movie. It'll shoot in Pennsylvania for six weeks. Pre-production starts in two weeks. I want you to be the line producer."

She no longer heard the rain or the wind because suddenly the room became quiet. All she could hear was her heartbeat echoing in her ears. This was what she'd worked for, dreamed of, all her adult life. And Peters had offered her the job with the same enthusiasm he used for asking her to get him a cup of coffee. She realized her mouth was open, so she shut it.

"Well?" He wasn't smiling or pleased for her, just impatient.

Her first impulse was to scream yes, but a thought flashed through her mind before the word came out. What about Luke? Maybe this was the break she'd been praying for. Perhaps they wouldn't have to go their separate ways . . . at least not so soon. As the producer, she could put him on her show. That is, if it had special effects.

She struggled to make her voice sound normal. "What's the picture about?"

"Life in a company town . . . steel mills, the local union, a family struggling to make it in the recession."

In the most blase tone she could muster, she asked, "Will it be all interiors and dialogue?"

He turned in his chair and stared straight at her. "No. We'll need special effects."

Her blush started at her toes and raced up to the top of her head. Smooth move, she thought. Subtle, and with great finesse. The very edge of Peters' mouth curved slightly upward. It was the first smile she'd ever seen on his ever-placid face.

After a deep breath, she went on. "I'll need to get back to you on this, boss. I'd love to do it, but I have some personal business I have to get straight first."

He was no longer looking at her, but was engrossed, once again, in his work. "Fine. Just make sure you let me know before the end of the week. I have a few people waiting in the wings if you decide not to go."

"I'll let you know tomorrow."

A sound that was a cross between a grunt and a cough was his only reply.

She looked down at the papers on her desk, but her mind was racing with plans. She would tell Luke tonight, and ask him if he would join her on the shoot. Of course, he would, she told herself. He does care about me.

A producer! The title reverberated in her head. If only she were alone, she would call her parents. They would be so pleased and proud of her. It meant more responsibility and more money. Of course, Peters would be the executive producer and she would still have to report to him, but as far as the day-to-day running of the set, she would be the boss. Who would the director be? Would it be inappropriate for her to share a room with Luke? He would flip when she told him.

A new series of thoughts stopped her excitement. The new position might be uncomfortable for Luke. They had never discussed this possibility. Being the associate producer was still close to being one of the crew. But when you were the line producer, it was crystal clear that you were in a whole different class, and everyone involved treated you differently.

She would only be invited to gatherings out of courtesy. If something went wrong, she would be the one the crew complained to, battled with. Even though she and Luke would be working together, they would be miles apart in terms of power and prestige.

Certainly it wouldn't matter, she told herself. Luke wasn't that narrow-minded. He would be proud of her, just as she was proud of the work he did. With his love of special effects, he would be the first person to understand her passion for achieving her best, just as he was determined to be the best in the business. Each of them could be on top of their chosen fields, and have the added bonus of working together. Not many couples could claim that.

To her surprise, she realized that being a ''couple'' with Luke was just as important to her as being a producer. Thinking about their night together, after her painful confession, warmed her all over again. He was so different from Craig. For the first time in her life, she felt as though she could begin to trust a man.

This relationship was quite bewildering. No proof was needed, no rationalizing away selfish behavior, no conditions whatsoever. The one thing she could count on from Luke was that he would tell her the truth.

"Catlin."

The voice startled her and she came back to the present. Peters was standing in front of her, holding out the board. His face was red, and he'd obviously been trying to get her attention for a while. She swallowed, then smiled up at him with beguiling innocence.

"Yes?"

"If it wouldn't be too much trouble, we have to discuss the fire scenes. That is, if you're not too busy."

"That's what I like about you, Mr. Peters. You have such an interesting sense of humor."

He stopped glaring after a few moments, and they were able to get to work. They began the discussion where she and Luke had left off . . . would the budget permit the burning of the slave shacks in addition to the fire at the plantation house? It would mean going over budget and keeping two of the most expensive stars for an additional three days.

Besides, she thought, if she were to approve spending all that money for Luke's project, Peters would assume she did it because they were lovers. And she couldn't afford to rock the boat . . . not now.

They wouldn't burn the shacks, just the main house. Relief washed over her at his final words. But as Peters left to go back to the motel, Catlin was unsettled. Was she being fair to Luke?

"I'll take the job," Luke yelled into the portable phone. "Give me two weeks to wrap here, then I'll need another week back home. Send the ticket to my place in Colorado. You have the address? Good. Okay, Jacques. We'll talk later. Bye."

"Who was that?" Sylvia sat perched on the tailgate of Bessie, eating her sandwich and eavesdropping.

"You are nosey, aren't you?" Luke grabbed a soda from his tiny refrigerator and sat next to his old friend.

"Yes, I am. It's what gives me pleasure in life. So, tell me who was on the phone."

"I got my next picture. And it shoots in Paris, France."

"Oh, my goodness. That's wonderful. Do they have someone for wardrobe?"

Luke stared at her, marveling at her gall. "They're only taking a few Americans on this shoot. I'm not sure about wardrobe, but I doubt they'll want to fly you over."

"Well, what makes you so special, monsieur?"

"It's a horror flick, but very high class. They want the effects to work in the States, so they're importing the best."

"And the most modest."

"Look who's talking."

"When you're my age, you have to be proud of something," Sylvia said with a laugh. "What about Stan?"

Luke's smile faded. "Can't afford to take him. I'll set him up with another job before I leave. And pray that he doesn't like his new boss better than me. I want him back.''

''You might lose a lot more than Stan, you know,'' she said quietly.

Luke stared at her, knowing exactly what she was referring to. Catlin had been on his mind all morning. He hadn't been able to shake last night's conversation. His logical side kept telling him that the only possible choice he had was to leave the relationship where it belonged . . . as a location romance, pure and simple.

But there was another side, a voice that he'd never heard before, telling him he'd be the biggest fool that ever lived if he left that woman behind.

That phone call put an end to his indecision.

''Don't you worry your pretty little head about Catlin. She knows the score. Besides, why would she want to get tangled up with a guy like me? I'm just the effects man, sweetheart. And Catlin's on her way to much bigger and better things.'' He smiled, a little too widely. ''Now, don't you go running off at the mouth. I don't want everyone in the crew to come begging for a job in Paris, got it?''

''I'll be quiet. I just hope you know what you're doing.''

''Me too, doll. Me, too.''

''Hey, sailor, you know where a girl can have a good time around here?''

Luke spun around and grinned, instantly wrapping Catlin in his arms and hugging her tightly to him. ''There's the cot.''

She looked at the bed, covered with bits and pieces of metal, wood, and wire. It was particularly uninviting from an aesthetic point of view, but it made her smile because it was just like Luke to overlook the obvious and see only the romantic side of things.

She shook her head. "How about tonight? We should be wrapping pretty early. If you come by after eight, I'll cook you dinner."

Still holding her close, he nuzzled her neck, creating goosebumps up and down her body. "I don't want to wait until eight," he whispered. The warm air on her ear made her shiver deliciously.

"Isn't it good that one of us is practical? Call me crazy, but making love in the middle of a truck in full view of the crew isn't my idea of the perfect date."

"You didn't think it was crazy in the slave shack."

She pushed herself out of his arms. "That was different."

"Why?" His mouth was serious, but his eyes were laughing.

"You know perfectly well that no one was going to be near that shack. Now, be a good boy and let me get back to work so I can get out of here when the rest of the crew wraps."

"Yes, ma'am."

But instead of letting her go, he grabbed her again and kissed her, running his hands down her back to her buttocks and squeezing her tight against the hardness of his body. She closed her eyes and let his tongue work its magic, abandoning herself to the forbidden sensations his intimate hold wrested from her. When he released her, she was breathless.

TEN

Luke arrived too early. The salad wasn't tossed, the candles weren't lit, and her hair was a disaster. Catlin debated telling him to come back later, but she was anxious to see him.

"Come in."

She hurriedly struck a match and brought it to the long, slender candle before she looked up. When she did, the match was forgotten. He was dressed in the most exquisite suit she'd ever seen. Gray with black pin striping, the jacket fit his body as if tailored by a lover. The lapels were narrow and formed a curved vee over the white, high-collared shirt, which was unbroken by a necktie. His pants draped elegantly down his long legs, all the way to his . . . tennis shoes! She started to laugh, but then the forgotten flame reached her fingertip and she flung the match on the table.

"Ouch!" She put her finger to her lips to cool the burn.

Luke took her hand and placed her fingers in his mouth. He slowly explored the soft pads of flesh with his tongue.

"Oh, my," she said. The dinner flew from her mind, the candles were ignored, and all that existed was the warm, wet feeling of incredible intimacy that made her nipples harden and her insides go liquid. No one had ever sucked her fingers before. She never wanted anyone else to perform this sensual delight.

When he finally released her hand, she saw that he was carrying a bouquet of flowers, at least two dozen long-stemmed white roses. Their beauty was overshadowed in her mind by his thoughtfulness. He'd obviously gone to as much trouble as she had for this impromptu dinner. She touched a rose and silently promised to press it in her photo album so she could remember this night forever.

"They're gorgeous," she said.

"I'm glad you like them." He handed them to her, and while she looked around the room as if a vase would suddenly appear from nowhere, he said, "Hold on, I'll be right back."

He dashed outside, and quickly returned holding a milk carton. He went to the bathroom sink, poured the milk down the drain, grabbed a knife from the counter and cut the top off of the plastic container, then rinsed it out and filled it with tap water.

"I figured you wouldn't have a vase *after* I bought the flowers. This is all I could come up with."

"It'll work beautifully. Elegant, but not overstated."

For the first time since he arrived, Luke looked around the room. His eyes widened at the sight of the mushrooms sautéing in the popcorn popper and the filet mignon sizzling on the tiny hibachi.

"Everything looks great. What's in there?" He pointed to the covered pot on the hot plate.

"Wild rice."

"Yum. What can I do to help?"

"Just open the wine. I have a few more things to do, then we can eat."

"At your service, madam."

He took the bottle of Beaujolais and sat at the table. Catlin scurried around the room, finishing the salad, preparing the plates, finally lighting the candles. She passed by the bathroom mirror and caught a glimpse of her disheveled hair. She slammed the door shut and furiously brushed and tucked until she looked passable. Next to Luke, she felt like Jo-Jo the Dogfaced Boy, but it was the best she could do. At least her dress was still clean and her pantyhose had no runs.

She thought of the news she was going to tell him, and was thrilled all over again. The trick was finding just the right moment. She took a deep breath, opened the door, and went to join him.

Luke was sipping his wine, looking relaxed and handsome at the small table. It only took a few minutes to serve the food and sit down next to him. Her appetite had been lost somewhere between fixing the salad dressing and brushing her hair, so she watched him as he dug in.

"This is fabulous," he said. "My first home-cooked meal in months. How did you figure all this out?" He pointed to the eclectic assortment of cooking devices.

"I tried to think like a special effects supervisor. I wanted the dinner to be wonderful, so I used a little creativity."

He took her hand and stroked the palm with his thumb. "I like that in a woman."

She batted her eyelashes. "Oh, golly."

"Speaking of effects, I wanted to go over the burning of the slave shacks with you. I've got some interesting ideas."

Her breath caught in her throat. Peters had obviously not told Luke that the stunt was off. She would have to break the news to him.

"Oh, Luke, I'm sorry, but we went over the board today and decided that we couldn't do any additional scenes."

He let go of her hand, took his napkin from his lap, and patted his mouth. His muscles grew tight around his jaw. It was obvious that he hadn't expected to be turned down, and she silently cursed Peters for leaving the dirty work to her.

"*We* decided?" he asked. "Just two days ago, Peters was all for it."

"He . . . reconsidered." Why was this so awkward? Her decision had been good business.

"What was your vote?" He looked at her now with questioning eyes.

"Luke, it wasn't anything personal. It's a matter of dollars and cents. I simply couldn't allow us to go so much over budget."

"Wait a minute." The hurt turned to anger before her eyes. "You mean to tell me that it was *you* that squashed this?"

All guilt stopped when she heard his accusatory tone. "Yes. Me. That's my job." Her stomach was in knots. Couldn't he see the logic of her position?

"Your job? That's the important thing, isn't it? Don't you think I realized that it would have a financial impact?'' he fired at her. "It wasn't just a whim on my part. I don't go around suggesting new scenes so I can look good. The fire as it exists misses the mark. It'll look like a cheap TV movie the way it's planned now, but with the addition of the shacks it could've looked great . . . like a theatrical piece, and not something for the small screen.''

"That's not the point. I'm sure it would look great, but we have just so much money, and I can't go over budget. Especially not now. . . .''

Luke stood up abruptly causing his chair to topple backwards and hit the curtained window behind him. He didn't seem to notice. "Money. Don't you care about the integrity of the show? It's always going to be over budget, there's never enough cash. You're supposed to fight to make the picture the best it can be. If it's only about money, you should work in a bank.''

Shaking with anger, she flew out of her seat. "How dare you? You don't know the half of it. I've struggled all along on this show, stealing from one department to boost something else. I've squeezed every penny I could so that it would show up on the screen. Have you already forgotten the thousand I gave you for your precious "big bang"? Her voice grew low, but the fury inside her still mounted even while she fought to retain some semblance of calm. "I really resent your accusations, Luke. You're speaking without thinking, and saying things you can't possibly mean.''

He walked around the table until he was directly in front of her, put his hands on her shoulders, and looked into her face. His eyes were like flint and his fingers dug into her flesh.

"I don't understand how you could have made this decision without talking to me first. That's what hurts. I thought you were on my side." His words were just above a whisper, but they cut through her like a knife.

He dropped his hands and they stood like two islands separated by miles of sea. She wanted to grab him and tell him that he was wrong, that she *was* on his side, that she would never do anything to hurt him. But she couldn't shut out the voice that kept repeating that he was right. She hadn't discussed it with him.

She'd been so anxious not to let their personal relationship damage her standing with Peters that she'd vetoed Luke's plans without truly considering his position. She'd used her power to get what she wanted, and had undercut the man she loved.

"Luke. . . ." Catlin stopped speaking when she heard the rapping on her front door. He turned to open it, and her hand went out to stop him.

"Wait."

He didn't stop. Sylvia was standing outside, holding a bottle of wine and a large bag of potato chips. Her smile faded when she saw the look on Luke's face.

"I can come back later."

"No, it's fine," he said tightly. "I was just leaving." He turned to Catlin. "I forgot to tell you. I've got my next picture lined up." His lips pressed tightly together and he shook his head slowly. "In Paris."

Catlin's heart hit the ground as she watched him walk out the door. She felt as if she'd just been struck by a cannonball. She tried to smile at her friend, but her lips wouldn't cooperate. "This really isn't the best time, Sylvia. I'm sorry. I'd love to talk, but right now. . . ."

"I kind of figured," said Sylvia. "No sweat, next time I'll call first."

Catlin walked outside and put her arm around the small woman. "Thanks." She looked past Sylvia's shoulder, and her pulse raced as she watched Luke climb into the cab of his truck, slam the door, and peel out of the parking lot. She released her hold and stood watching the truck turn the corner and drive out of view.

"Could you use a friendly ear? And maybe some strong drink?"

Catlin looked at the bottle, the chips, and the warm smile that were being offered. "You know, I think I could. Come on in."

Sylvia looked at the nearly full dinner plates, then at Catlin. "Well, the fight couldn't have been about your cooking. This stuff smells great."

Catlin laughed, although she felt as if there was nothing funny in the whole world. "No, I wish it were about food. If you're hungry, help yourself. It's still warm."

"Thanks, I will." She sat down, but didn't lift a fork.

Catlin didn't know what to do, what to think. "I've made such a huge mistake. And I think I'm going to pay for it for a long time. I don't know why I ever let Luke McKeever into my life."

"It's not hard to see why." Sylvia poured two glasses of wine and tore open the bag of chips. She sat forward on her chair and waited for Catlin to settle on the bed. "He's quite a guy, even if he can be a world-class idiot sometimes."

"No. He's not the idiot. He told me from the start that he wouldn't stick around. But somehow I didn't see this coming. Not like this."

"Yeah. It wasn't the nicest exit line I've ever heard."

Catlin took a healthy swig of her wine before she responded. "It was my fault. I knew he was going to leave. And what did I do as a final, loving gesture? I killed his pet project. Not because of money or the schedule, but because I thought it might look bad. 'Cause, now here's the real joke, Peters offered me a job as producer. Funny, huh? I got what I wanted, then got scared that someone might think I was using my position to play favorites."

"Honey, no one would have given it a second thought . . . except you."

"I know that . . . up here." She pointed to her head. "But all I could think of was that Peters would take back the offer. And then I'd lose Luke forever."

"What do you mean?"

"I had it all planned. See, I was gonna offer him a job. In my stupid, optimistic dreams I thought that if I could just make sure we worked together, that would be the answer. We'd go on and on in a location romance that would never end. But all I've managed to do is make sure he never wants to speak to me again."

As soon as she closed the door behind Sylvia, the tears started. Once they began, there was no holding them back. She ran to the bed and flung herself on the spread. Waves of pain washed over her until she felt she would drown. With great effort she took deep breaths and calmed down a bit.

After what seemed like hours, she grew silent. The pain was constant and growing familiar. She had to make a decision. Should she go to Luke, and try to explain? Or should she cut her losses and learn to live with the emptiness that was once her heart?

Luke gazed at the murky water of the Mississippi. The storm-tossed waves reflected the turbulence of his emotions. Damn her, he thought. Damn women, damn love. He shifted on the leather seat of his truck, trying to ease the aching muscles of his back. The heater beckoned, but he didn't turn it on. The punishing cold was appropriate. Maybe she's right, he thought. It was just a movie, for God's sake, not brain surgery. What difference did it make if he burned the slave shacks? No one would ever know.

He would know.

The gray haze of morning moved gently over the water, and still he sat in his truck. After he'd left Catlin, he'd driven aimlessly until he'd reached a quiet spot. Nothing but trees and river to surround him in his anger. Hour after hour had gone by, but the resentment hadn't dissipated.

Now, it was finally time to look beyond the obvious and admit what was *really* bothering him. He turned on the ignition and cranked up the heater. The first blast of air was chilly, but after a few minutes the cab warmed, and his hold on his fury eased.

Was his anger just about the fire, or was it an excuse to run away and never have to confront his feelings about Catlin?

God, he didn't want to look at that. He'd always

thought of himself as a man who faced the consequences of his actions. But he hadn't counted on Cat. He'd never expected to fall in love. Not with a woman who was as intent on success as she was. Not again.

He'd been reporting his expenditures to Catlin since she'd started, but he hadn't really thought about what that meant. Of course, he knew she was the associate producer, but that title could mean anything. He'd known some who had never even been on a set. But she wasn't that kind of producer. She took her job seriously and did it well. One of the things he admired about her was her quickness, her obvious capability. But now her talents had a direct impact on him. She would be moving up to producer while he would remain effects supervisor.

He'd always been so proud of that title. Now he felt as if he was just another cog in the below-the-line machinery of making movies. And if his word didn't mean anything, if she was going to just make blanket decisions without talking to him about it, well, then he *was* just a drone.

Luke slammed his open palms onto the steering wheel, then held them pressed against the plastic with such force that he felt his shaking hands would bleed.

What the hell had happened? What could she have been thinking? He'd have to explain that in his realm of special effects, he was king. No one from the front office had any business dismissing him like so much dust on a coffee table.

Hell, what good would it do for him to explain? They were all wrong for each other, and that was the bottom line. The smartest thing he could do would be to forget about her. To go on to Paris and have a ball.

His gaze went back to the wide expanse of water winding its way effortlessly toward the ocean. Then why did he feel as if something vital inside him had just gone forever?

"I'll take that job in Pennsylvania. But I want to leave immediately."

Catlin stood outside the door of Peters' motel room. It was early, barely six o'clock. Peters was still in his robe. He stared at her for a moment, as if she'd spoken Swahili.

"Mr. Peters? I said, I'll take the. . . ."

"I heard you. I just can't figure out why you needed to tell me at six. And what's all this crap about you leaving immediately?"

"This show is almost finished. The board's complete and the paperwork's in. Everything else can be done by the assistant directors. And I wasn't going to work on post-production, anyway. I just feel I can be of more use on the next show. I can scout, line up the local unions, get hotels. . . ."

"Yeah, I know what a producer does." His face remained implacable. "When do you want to go?"

She swallowed. "Today."

"Okay."

That was it? Just, okay? The man would never cease to amaze her. "Thanks, Mr. Peters. You won't regret it."

"Yeah."

She had to speak quickly, or he would shut the door. "And there's something else."

A blink. She took that to mean he would listen.

"I was wrong about burning the slave shacks. I went over the script and made the necessary changes last night. I don't believe it will cost us that much money and the effort will be worth it. All the paperwork is done, and, I promise, you won't miss the money. But you would miss how spectacular it's going to look when Luke gets finished."

He scowled. "You're pressing your luck."

"I know." All she could do was take her medicine.

"All right. Get me the approvals before you leave."

She turned away before he could change his mind. His voice stopped her.

"Don't you think it might help if you had a script for the new show?"

Blushing furiously, she went back to the door and waited while he dug out her copy of the Pennsylvania film. After a nod of thanks, she left.

The walk back to her room was slower than her approach had been. The air was colder and her jacket felt as if it was made of paper. Crossing her arms against the wind, she shivered. It was done. She could be packed and out of here before nightfall. She wouldn't have to see Luke at all.

The pain that had been mercifully dormant for a few minutes washed over her again. Why? The question had been burning in her mind all night. Why go to all the trouble of making her love him, if he were just going to leave? Had his ex-wife hurt him so badly that he needed to see some other woman suffer?

She laughed to herself. Pretty soon she would be trying to figure out why Craig had duped her. At least that pain was well-worn territory. There were no answers, except that she'd gotten herself into the very same mess, even after all her soul-searching and fervent promises. It had to be a character defect, one that would haunt her forever.

No more. Never again would she open up enough to let someone in. The only smart thing she'd ever done was pick a career that could consume her. And, she decided, she would jump back into that career with both feet.

Once in her room, she got right to work. She booked a flight for five P.M. That would give her just enough time to pack, finish up any last minute details at the trailer, and get to the airport.

She tuned the clock radio to a hard rock station and cranked up the volume. She didn't want to hear herself think. Then she picked up the roses, still poised in the milk carton, and tossed them in the trash.

Luke jumped down from the effects truck and rubbed his eyes. He could remember a time when the loss of one night's sleep hadn't fazed him. Those days were long gone. He felt like hell.

Peters had summoned him, and when the master called, he jumped. He couldn't help wondering if it had really been Catlin who'd sent for him. He wanted to see her, to tell her they needed to talk.

He hadn't stopped thinking about her. Even when he was concentrating on work, the questions bombarded him. Did he really want to go to Paris? Or was he just running away? Was there any chance that he and Catlin could make a go of it?

When he'd been with Susan, the problems had become larger and their love had diminished. In his heart, he knew that the love would have ended even without the difficulties. The marriage was over when they both realized that.

Catlin was a whole different story. The more he thought about her, the stronger his need for her became. So what if she had more power on the set? He would still be in charge of his department. He had a lot to be proud of there.

His gait quickened. He was actually anxious to see her. He reached the door of the producer's trailer and jumped inside. His heart fell when he saw Peters sitting alone. Oh, well, he'd find her soon.

"You wanted to see me?"

Peters looked up at him. His eyebrows came together and his mouth puckered as if he'd just licked a lemon. "The scene's in."

"What scene?"

"The fire scene. Burning the slave shacks. That's what you wanted to do, wasn't it?"

"Uh, yeah." He was stunned. "I was under the impression. . . ."

"I know. You were told one thing, now I'm telling you another." He held out some sheets of paper. "Here's the new shooting schedule. We do the fire tomorrow."

Peters had to rattle the papers before Luke could make his body move. He studied the neat typing without seeing anything. "Is Catlin around?"

The boss didn't answer. For a second, Luke thought he looked sort of perplexed, but that couldn't be. Peters was sure of *everything,* and most sure of what he didn't know. Finally, he said, "She's not here. She's left town."

"I don't get it. What's the joke?" There was an awful pressure squeezing his chest.

"Dammit, I hate this personal crap." Peters looked down and picked up his pen so Luke couldn't see his face. "I hired her as a producer on my next film. She left to scout. You have any problems with that, work it out on your own time. Got it?"

"Sure. Pardon me. Didn't mean to get human on you."

Luke was out the door before his clenched fist went through Peters' face. She had left town. No good-bye, nothing. One little argument and she was gone. Well, the hell with her. He'd be damned if he was going to miss her.

Then why did he feel as if he'd just been run over by a truck?

Catlin entered her hotel room and looked around the small space that would be her home for the next few months. Even though the room was well lit, had large windows, and the decor was cheerful, she felt as if there was a gray haze blanketing all she surveyed.

She drifted to the king-sized bed and sat down. The emptiness in her stomach could be hunger, since it had been almost twelve hours since she'd eaten, but food couldn't fill the hole that had settled there. She stared at the black television screen, not seeing, not caring.

The overwhelming feeling of being totally alone made her want to throw up. If this was the price of independence, then it was too high. It should have been a time for celebration. She'd reached a major goal in her life, she was a producer! Yet, all she wanted to do was cry.

The plane ride replayed in her mind as clearly as if she were watching it on the still-silent tube. Without realizing it, she'd expected him to stop her. Only when the plane took off did she admit that she'd desperately wanted Luke to be there . . . to take her in his arms, to kiss away her fears.

She'd even thought about going back to him. But that would've meant begging him to love her, and that was one thing she could never do. If she had nothing else, she still had her pride.

She tried to shake herself out of her lethargy. Glancing at her baggage, she groaned at the task ahead of her. It seemed like far too much work to unpack even one bag. All she wanted to do was crawl into bed and stay there until the aching in her chest had become bearable—or the pain killed her. After a heartfelt sigh, she rose and managed to put away the contents of her overnight case.

She slipped on her nightgown, then took out the new script and settled herself in the low, cushioned chair situated in front of a good lamp. The first few pages held her interest, then images of Luke started intruding . . . taunting images of happy times and loving words. Soon the script was forgotten and she was back in his arms. She pictured his face, his clear blue eyes dancing with delight as he held her, his lips curled in a devilish grin right before he kissed her.

The picture shattered as if the glass screen of the TV had exploded into a thousand tiny slivers that embedded in her soul. It was as if she'd damaged a part of herself that could never be fixed. An endless, anguished night loomed in front of her.

ELEVEN

Luke pointed the stream of fire from his torch onto the already charred metal. The gas pipes for the fire scene had to be perfect; safety always came first. Stan had offered to help, but he needed to work, needed to concentrate on something with his whole being. The fact that it had taken over sixteen hours to complete the job had been a blessing. But, just to be safe, he'd run a complete test in the morning to make sure he hadn't made any errors.

He turned off the torch and lifted the visor from his face. Sweat poured down his skin. After clearing his eyes with his sleeve, he looked around. Of course, he was alone. Everyone else had gone back to the motel hours ago. It was nearly midnight.

He longed for a shower and a clean bed. Now he could leave, now that every aching muscle screamed at him for sleep. There was no chance he would lie awake and think of her.

The day had been miserable. Everyone on the crew

knew about his relationship with Catlin and they had all been sickeningly nice to him all day. Considerate, polite. He wanted to punch their lights out.

He stored his gear and wearily climbed into his truck. As he drove the familiar streets back to the motel, he turned on the radio, loud, so that the noise would block his thoughts. But, dammit, they had to play that cowboy song he'd sung to her in Louisiana. He flipped off the switch and the silence of the night swallowed him.

Catlin. That stupid habit she had of playing with stray wisps of hair. Her eyes. The way they crinkled when she smiled at one of his awful jokes. And that body of hers. It was as if she'd been designed to fit him, like the missing piece of a jigsaw puzzle.

If only he could have turned that torch on his memories and burned them from his brain. But the memories wouldn't leave him. They replayed over and over like a broken record.

When he reached the motel, he walked to his room, stripped off his clothes and got under the shower. The water washed away the sweat and filth of work, but seemed to make his thoughts of Catlin clearer. The night she told him about Craig ran like a film through his mind. How he'd abandoned her, tricked her, made her feel like such a fool.

. He turned off the water. Hell, he'd only heard one side of the story. Maybe she'd turned tail and run from him, too. They'd probably had some fight about her career, she'd made up all sorts of garbage about him, and left him like a used-up rag.

He was rubbing himself so fiercely with the towel that his skin hurt. When he looked down, he saw angry red streaks along his flesh. It looked as if he'd been burned. How appropriate.

It was a struggle to keep his new image of her in mind. Every time he thought he had a fix on her, a picture of the Catlin he knew in his heart—beautiful and vulnerable—would intrude and he'd have to start all over again. In the end, he knew he could no longer pretend.

His bed held no comfort. It could have been made of rocks for all the ease his body felt. What was she doing now? Was she feeling any of the pain that was driving him insane? Or was she lying asleep, dreaming of how she'd gotten away . . . free and clear?

Catlin turned the light on. It was three A.M. and she was more miserable than she'd ever been in her life. The room was filled with unfriendly shadows and the sounds of the busy street filtering past the heavy glass windows in a conspiracy to keep her from getting any sleep.

She sat up, plumping her pillows behind her back, and picked up the telephone. The dial tone seemed too loud. She punched the numbers for room service and waited. Ring after ring echoed in her ears, but she didn't want to give up.

Surely someone would be in the restaurant. Anyone. Was a bottle of wine so much to ask for? If she could just have a little bit of liquor, she was sure she could get to sleep. But the phone kept ringing; the empty, impersonal sound of no one listening.

It was the nightmare, not the alarm that woke Luke up. A thin sheen of perspiration chilled him as the breeze from the open window washed over his body.

He struggled to control his quick, shallow breathing. The images still lingered just outside his consciousness.

Catlin had been trapped in a burning slave shack. He couldn't reach her—no matter what he did, he couldn't save her. Panic had stirred him into a frenzy. The feeling of helplessness made him sick.

He focused on his room, the chair, his rumpled clothes lying on the floor. He was back in reality, but still shaken. "Hell," he said. Then he got up to start his day.

Catlin finished her breakfast in the hotel dining room. Her day would be as busy as she could make it. The packed schedule was intentional because she didn't want time to think. She'd realized last night that she hadn't called her parents. They didn't know about the new job, or that she was in Pennsylvania. She must call, but it was going to be hard to appear enthusiastic. Her mother would figure out something was wrong, and she'd want to talk about it. Catlin didn't think she could bear it. Her mind was too occupied with Mississippi. . . .

Today was a big day of shooting in Natchez—the fire scene. No matter how she tried to block it out, she couldn't help worrying about Luke and thinking about what would happen to him.

The final test on the gas pipes completed, Luke and Stan put the finishing touches on the slave shacks. The whole area had been roped off by the crew and the fire department. Even though they had done hundreds of fires before, there was always a sharp tension before a big stunt. Something could always go wrong. Luke's job was to make sure nothing did. He had even paid Brandon and his buddies to keep clear. That money had been out of his own pocket, but worth it for the peace of mind it gave him.

He walked around the shacks for the last time. Everything appeared to be in order. The cameras were set up a safe distance away, the stunt people had insulated suits under their clothes, and the fire hoses were in place and ready to go. Now, he would talk to the director, then they would set this world on fire.

Catlin looked at her watch. Twelve-thirty. Were the fires lit? Was Luke being careful? She should have stayed. At least she would have known he was safe. So many things could go wrong. The thought of Luke being hurt or. . . .

It was almost time for her second meeting. How was she going to concentrate? All that was supposed to matter was her job. Luke was someone in her past. She had no business worrying so much about him. He obviously hadn't worried about her. But, dammit, the pain wasn't easing in her heart. She longed for him with all of her being. The honest truth was, she wanted to get on the next plane to Natchez and be with him. Beg him to take her back. Even her precious career didn't seem to matter much when she was faced with a life without Luke.

But what about her pride?

"We're all set, Mr. Peters," Luke said, wiping his brow with a towel. "Everything's a go."

"Fine."

Luke turned away from his boss, and was already

picturing each step of the fire in his mind when he felt Peters' hand on his arm.

"It was Catlin who did this."

Luke stopped. For a moment he wasn't sure he heard correctly. "What?"

Peters sighed with impatience. "It was your friend that got this scene on the boards. Before she left."

Luke was stunned. "You mean. . . ."

"What part of the sentence didn't you understand? It was her call, and she made sure you got your fire scene. I just hope she was right."

"She was," Luke said. "It's gonna be worth every penny."

"Yeah, that's what she said. Now, prove it to me." Peters walked away.

"Why didn't she say anything?" Luke said out loud. "I don't get it."

"Don't get what?"

Stan was beside him.

"Nothing," Luke said, walking back toward the house. "I told Peters we were ready to go."

Stan nodded. "Yep. All set." He walked in silence until they reached the wide porch. "Did he tell you about Catlin?"

Luke tripped on the front step, but managed to catch himself before he fell. "What?"

"You know, that it was because of her that we're lighting up the shacks."

Luke looked at his young partner. His face was innocence itself. "How did you know?"

"Jeez, dude. Everyone knew. But you."

Luke shook his head and walked into the house. He needed time to think.

*   *   *

Catlin paced across the small motel room. The preliminary contracts at the rental agency hadn't been ready. The meeting was rescheduled for Tuesday. The rest of the day and the long weekend stretched in front of her like an unbroken expanse of desert. If she stayed in her room, she would go mad.

After a quick shower, she called for room service. She wasn't the least bit hungry, but it would give her something to do. She couldn't rest, couldn't read . . . all she could do was think about Luke. She'd call Peters. He would tell her how the last shot had gone.

She hung up after the fifteenth ring. Obviously, everyone was at the fire. It was nearly four. It should have been over by now. Unless something had gone wrong.

Fear shot through her. A dread that had no name, no rhyme, no reason. But she trusted the feeling—as much as she'd trusted anything in her life—as much as she loved and needed Luke. *Oh God, please don't let anything be wrong.* With shaking fingers, she pulled the phone book from the drawer of the nightstand. She held the directory, unopened, on her lap.

Her heart slowed from its frantic beating as she pictured Luke, heard him tell her he loved her. He had to be okay because she had a job to do. She had to make him see that they were meant to be together. In a moment of startling clarity, she knew that her pride had nearly cost her the one thing that mattered most in the world . . . the man she loved.

She dialed the number for Southeast Airlines.

Luke put the torch to the stream of invisible gas and heard the whoosh of fire before he saw the flames. In seconds, the first shack was an inferno. Everything was going according to plan. Stuntmen were running, screaming, out of the burning building. Then the other shacks went up in flames. The heat was becoming unbearable. His gaze flicked from one building to the next. He wanted to see everything all at once and make sure there were no mistakes.

A flash of brown . . . where there should've only been fire. What was it? He ran around the perimeter of the barrier and peered into the back of the fourth shack. There it was again. It wasn't his imagination. Someone was caught in the burning building!

Luke couldn't see. The smoke filled his lungs and burned his eyes. He felt the hair on his arms smolder. What was that? He ducked as a burning timber fell with a deafening crash inches from where he stood. He'd lost it again . . . no. There was the brown shirt. It was a boy! Oh, Christ, it was Brandon. He ran, stumbling through hell.

Luke grabbed the boy's arm and pulled, bringing the terrified child close to his chest. "It's okay," he screamed. "I'll get you out of here."

They couldn't go out the way he'd come in. Luke's body was racked with another coughing spasm. If he didn't move fast, they'd both be dead. He picked Brandon up and ran for the back wall. There was a space. He ducked under another falling beam. The wall. It wasn't completely burned yet.

He hauled the boy over his left shoulder and ran at the only space he could find. Turning so that his right side would get the brunt of the crash, he hit the boards with every ounce of his strength. Agonizing pain shot through his body as he broke through the barrier that trapped them.

Cool air filled his lungs and he realized dazedly that they'd made it. Someone took Brandon from him as he staggered and fell, exhausted, to the ground.

People were all around, firemen, crew members. An oxygen mask was over his mouth and he fought to fill his lungs with pure, clean air. Brandon was surrounded by paramedics and firemen. He saw the boy move, and nearly wept with relief.

Red-hot pain seared him. His arms and legs felt as though they were still on fire. Even the slight breeze brushing against the red flesh caused him to grit his teeth. He barely felt the needle as the paramedic gave him a shot, then the world went dark.

Luke opened his eyes reluctantly. The glare of the white walls hurt, so he closed them again. His arms were bandaged and hard to move, as were his legs. It wasn't that they were painful, he was still too drugged to feel that, but they felt heavy, uncomfortable. He shifted his body and changed his mind about how drugged he was. It hurt like hell.

His tongue felt like the track at the Indy 500 after a race. How was he supposed to ring for the nurse when moving his arms was so excruciating? He'd been dreaming about Catlin, and the soft words she'd spoken had been soothing, loving. If he woke up, she'd be gone and he'd have to face a pain-filled world alone.

There was a straw at his lips and he grasped it between his teeth gratefully, taking long gulps of water into his parched throat.

"Whoa, not so fast. You'll get sick."

That voice. His eyes flew open. Catlin stood beside his bed, holding the glass up to him. She was the most beautiful thing he'd ever seen. Her dark hair swirled around her face like a mahogany cloud, her lips parted slightly and he could see the edges of her white teeth. Her green eyes filled with concern and, yes, love.

"You're gonna be fine, sweetheart. The burns are only first and second degree. You won't even have scars."

He let go of the straw. "What. . . ." he croaked. His throat ached brutally.

"Shhh, my darling. Don't talk. The smoke irritated your throat." She brushed his lips with her fingers, and her touch was as soothing to his soul as the water had been to his body.

She was smiling, but tears were threatening to break free. He wanted to tell her that he'd be fine. Now that she was there. All he could do was smile back, and hope she would get the message.

"I guess I have a captive audience." She sniffed once, and a single tear spilled and slowly trickled down her soft cheek. "I'm probably making a complete fool of myself, but I don't care. About Paris. . . ." She took a deep breath before going on in a rush. "Take me with you. I love you, Luke, more than anything in the world. I'll quit my job, I'll find work in Europe, only don't leave me. You're all that matters to me now. I know you don't want anyone to tie you down, but I won't, I promise. You can do whatever you want, and I won't say a word. I was going to ask you to come with me to Pennsylvania, but when I got there I realized that it didn't matter where we were, just so long as we're together. I care more about you than any job, Luke. *Any* job."

She took a long deep breath before she continued.

"I know you like me, and maybe you could learn to love me . . . as much as I love you."

Her face was filled with so much pain and love that he would have paid a million dollars for arms that could hold and comfort her. Why did he have to lose his voice now? He shook his head and tried to make her see that she was all wrong. She was crying hard, and had buried her face in her hands. He held his breath and slowly lifted one bandaged arm until the white cloth reached her hand.

She gasped and looked at him. It took a minute to lower his arm and recover from the movement. Carefully, he mouthed each word so she would be sure to understand.

"I . . . love . . . you."

Luke watched Catlin while she slept, curled up like a kitten, in the chair beside his bed. She had been up most of the last two nights tending to him, and she'd finally collapsed in the hour before dawn. It was difficult to remember all of what had gone on because of the painkillers they had filled him with. But he knew that every time he'd moved or groaned or opened his eyes, Catlin had been there. If she wasn't making sure his thirst was quenched, then she was wiping his brow with a cool washcloth. But mostly she was loving him.

Each time their eyes met, he'd felt safe and complete. She was his. Whatever problems faced them, they would meet them together; he was determined that no job, no fear would keep them apart. Now, in her slumber, he could see how very vulnerable she was. For all her quick thinking and knowledge of their crazy business, she was still a very human, very tender woman. He could easily spend the rest of his life taking care of her.

As much as he wanted her to rest right now, a more urgent problem was making him shift uncomfortably on the bed. He tried to reach the nurse's call button, but his bandaged hands jerked awkwardly and the plastic buzzer clattered to the ground.

"What?" Catlin said, concern making her voice sound sharp. "Are you all right?"

She was on her feet and next to him in an instant.

"I'm . . . fine." His throat still felt scratchy, but it didn't hurt like it had yesterday.

"You talked!" Her eyes lit up with excitement. She bent over and kissed him lightly on the cheek. How he wanted to grab her and hold her next to him, to feel her body and her desire. But for now, all he could do was accept her loving gestures and make plans to repay her in kind.

"Do you want some water?" She rubbed the sleep out of her eyes, then made sure his glass was full.

"Not right now. I need to get rid of some. Desperately."

"Oh. I'll call the nurse." She found the fallen box and pushed the button. "I think I'll freshen up a bit, too."

As soon as her reinforcement came, Catlin went down the hall to wash up. Now that Luke could talk, she was frightened. What if he didn't want her? He'd said he loved her, but he was filled with drugs and in terrible pain. People said crazy things when they hurt. She closed the restroom door and leaned her head against the cool tile. Please, God, she prayed, let him love me.

At the basin, she turned on the water with shaking

ands. She looked awful. She hadn't taken time to shower for the past two days. Thank goodness for the nurses. They'd let her stay right next to him constantly. They'd even fed her. The soap and water refreshed her some, but now she had to face Luke.

When she came back, he was settled in comfortably. Her heart gave a little jolt when he smiled at her. She sat at the edge of his bed.

"How you doin', cowboy?"

"I got the world on a string, sittin' on a rainbow. . . ." His pathetic attempt to sing while his throat was still swollen made both of them wince.

"I don't think you're ready for Carnegie Hall yet, but it's great to see you in such good spirits," she said. "Do you hurt?"

He shook his head. "Nothing I can't take. It just feels like a whopper of a sunburn. I've felt worse."

She placed her hand on his chest and drew large lazy circles over the thin hospital gown. "Do you remember what we talked about the other night?"

Luke heard the fear in her voice, and his body responded to her touch. He was at a distinct disadvantage. Limited to a shaky voice and eyes still lulled by medication, he struggled to make her understand his feelings. "Honey, I can't fold you up in my arms, like I want to, so you'll have to listen with your heart."

Her hand grew still, and he could see tears well behind her thick lashes.

"I meant what I said about loving you," he said. "I meant more than that. You're more important to me than anything in this world, and I'm a jackass for not doing something about it sooner."

"But. . . ."

"Don't interrupt me. You'll have time to speak your piece later. I don't know why I took that job in Paris. I thought it was because I didn't want a permanent relationship, but I don't believe that now. Cat, I was scared. Don't get me wrong, I loved you, probably from the first moment I saw you, but I was carrying a lot of baggage. You know, my marriage didn't turn out so great."

His throat was getting uncomfortably raw. Catlin lifted the glass to his lips and he drank the cool water gratefully.

Her hand was unsteady as she put the glass down. "Maybe we should talk later. You should rest."

"No. I need to tell you, now." He fought to capture her gaze once again, and only when he had, did he continue. "Baby, I was scared I'd mess up again. The idea of you being my boss made me damned uncomfortable. But you know, after the hell I went through when you left, I don't care if you end up running the whole studio. I need you."

That was it. Catlin couldn't hold on any longer; tears fell down her cheeks and she didn't even try to stop them. "Oh, God, Luke. What *I* went through, thinking you didn't love me or want me. I nearly died." She lay her head on his chest, trying not to hurt him, but needing to be close.

His bandaged arms gently encircled her. "I'm glad."

Her head jerked up and she stared at him in disbelief.

"No, not that you were hurting," he said quickly. "I'm glad that once and for all we know that this isn't a location fling, but a forever romance."

She rested her cheek back down on his chest and sighed contentedly. "Oh, yes. Forever."

He couldn't see her face, but he felt her body stiffen slightly.

"Luke, I was so scared that you didn't love me that I jumped to all the wrong conclusions. I'm sorry. Now that we have each other, I want you to know that I meant what I said. I'll quit my job. We can go to Paris."

God, how he wanted to touch her. To ease her fears with his hands and his lips. "That will be nice, but we'll have to go after I finish my next job, because I turned the Paris gig down."

"What?" Catlin was afraid to look up.

"Harriet doesn't like French food. Besides, I got a better offer."

"What . . . kind of an offer?" Her voice was barely a whisper.

"I heard a producer needs me in Pennsylvania."

She couldn't speak. All she could do was hold the man she loved. And cry.

"Don't worry," he said. "I've heard Pittsburgh is a great place for a honeymoon. That is, if you don't mind marrying the special effects guy?"

"Darling," she said, looking up at him once again. "I'd be the happiest woman in the world if I were married to the special effects guy. Because the fire you lit in me will never go out."

Very carefully, she lifted herself until her lips could meet his, and she kissed him with all the love and joy she'd ever known.

EPILOGUE

Five years later . . .

Luke waved the chauffeur away and opened the limo door himself. He held out his hand and Catlin took hold of it. The smile she gave him as he helped her to the curb filled him with an overwhelming sense of peace. She was so beautiful, and she was his.

"How you doing, Mrs. McKeever?" he whispered into her ear.

"Wonderfully."

"And how about junior?" Luke reached for her belly, swollen in her eighth month of pregnancy. God, how he loved touching her, feeling the life inside her.

"Junior's just fine, but I think he's as nervous as I am. He's been practicing his dancing for the past half hour."

"You mean football." Luke laughed. "So, he's already affected by the business, hm?" He leaned a little closer to her tummy. "Don't worry, big guy. Even if we don't win this Emmy, there'll be plenty of trophies for you to play with."

He straightened and put his arm around his wife. "Ready?"

Catlin nodded. Nestled close to Luke, she accompanied him up the long red carpet leading to the auditorium where the technical achievement awards for excellence in television were to be awarded. Luke was up for two statuettes. Both for special effects on movies-of-the-week that she had produced.

Oh, there were other technical and artistic nominations for both shows, and she was thrilled about all of them, but nothing meant more to her than her husband's nominations. He was the best in his field, and she wasn't the only one who thought so.

As they made their way past the crowd of onlookers, *paparazzi,* celebrities, and the other nominees, she found herself thinking about the first time they'd worked together. It seemed like just yesterday they'd decided their love was too big to last for only one show. And how right they'd been.

The movie in Pennsylvania had been like a dream come true. Even the hectic wedding, held on the set during a lunch break, had been wonderful. The whole crew had gotten together to make their day a spectacular success. And as for a honeymoon? As far as she was concerned, it was still going on.

Luke found their seats at one of the hundred and fifty tables, and helped her into her chair. The sitting down part was easy. Getting up was a whole different story. She ran her hand over her stomach and felt the baby give her a kick.

Soon she would have a little boy, a little brother

for Katy. It amazed her that her daughter was already three, and as bright and pretty as a sunflower. Six movies and two children in five years. Quite an accomplishment.

Luke caught her attention, his blue eyes capturing her own in a glance that made her quiver. "Can I do anything for you? Get you some milk?"

"No, thanks, sweetheart. I'm fine."

He was so thoughtful, and such a wonderful father. It was Luke that had insisted they take Katy with them on the road. He'd set up everything from the baby-ready motor home to the nanny. And working together—it'd been better than either of them could have hoped.

She was an established producer now, still working for Peters. He sure hadn't changed in all this time, although he had been quite accommodating about taking Katy with them on location. She rarely saw him, nowadays. Their routine was an easy one, and he trusted her enough to give her free rein on the set. But he knew that the only films she wanted to produce were loaded with special effects.

The last two had been a real challenge: one a science fiction piece and the other a World War II drama. Luke had been in heaven. He'd worked extraordinarily hard, but he still had time each night to make sure she and Katy were comfortable and happy. It was, in fact, the best of both worlds.

Two awards, for costuming and editing, had already been given out. Next up was the Emmy for special effects. Catlin's heart started pounding. Oh, how she wanted him to win. Of course, having two of the five nominations helped, but she was still as nervous as a cat in a room full of rocking chairs.

". . . and the winner is . . ."

She grabbed Luke's hand and squeezed.

". . . Luke McKeever for *Eye of the Storm*."

Applause broke out all around them, and she thought her heart would burst. He stood, leaned over and kissed her.

"I love you," he said. Then he was off to shine in his moment in the spotlight.

It was right, she thought. Her handsome, talented husband should be awarded for special effects—for he'd always have the most incredible special effect on her.

SHARE THE FUN . . .
SHARE YOUR NEW-FOUND TREASURE!!

You don't want to let your new books out of your sight? That's okay. Your friends can get their own. Order below.

No. 43 DUET by Patricia Collinge
Adam & Marina fit together like two perfect parts of a puzzle!

No. 44 DEADLY COINCIDENCE by Denise Richards
J.D.'s instincts tell him he's not wrong; Laurie's heart says trust him.

No. 45 PERSONAL BEST by Margaret Watson
Nick is a cynic; Tess, an optimist. Where does love fit in?

No. 46 ONE ON ONE by JoAnn Barbour
Vincent's no saint but Loie's attracted to the devil in him anyway.

No. 47 STERLING'S REASONS by Joey Light
Joe is running from his conscience; Sterling helps him find peace.

No. 48 SNOW SOUNDS by Heather Williams
In the quiet of the mountain, Tanner and Melaine find each other again.

No. 49 SUNLIGHT ON SHADOWS by Lacey Dancer
Matt and Miranda bring out the sunlight in each other's lives.

No. 50 RENEGADE TEXAN by Becky Barker
Rane lives only for himself—that is, until he meets Tamara.

Meteor Publishing Corporation
Dept. 692, P. O. Box 41820, Philadelphia, PA 19101-9828

Please send the books I've indicated below. Check or money order (U.S. Dollars only)—no cash, stamps or C.O.D.s (PA residents, add 6% sales tax). I am enclosing $2.95 plus 75¢ handling fee for *each* book ordered.

Total Amount Enclosed: $_____.

___ No. 94	___ No. 33	___ No. 39	___ No. 45
___ No. 28	___ No. 34	___ No. 40	___ No. 46
___ No. 29	___ No. 35	___ No. 41	___ No. 47
___ No. 30	___ No. 36	___ No. 42	___ No. 48
___ No. 31	___ No. 37	___ No. 43	___ No. 49
___ No. 32	___ No. 38	___ No. 44	___ No. 50

Please Print:
Name _____
Address _____ Apt. No. _____
City/State _____ Zip _____

Allow four to six weeks for delivery. Quantities limited.